Eliza

Gary S. Park

Copyright 2024 by Gary S. Park

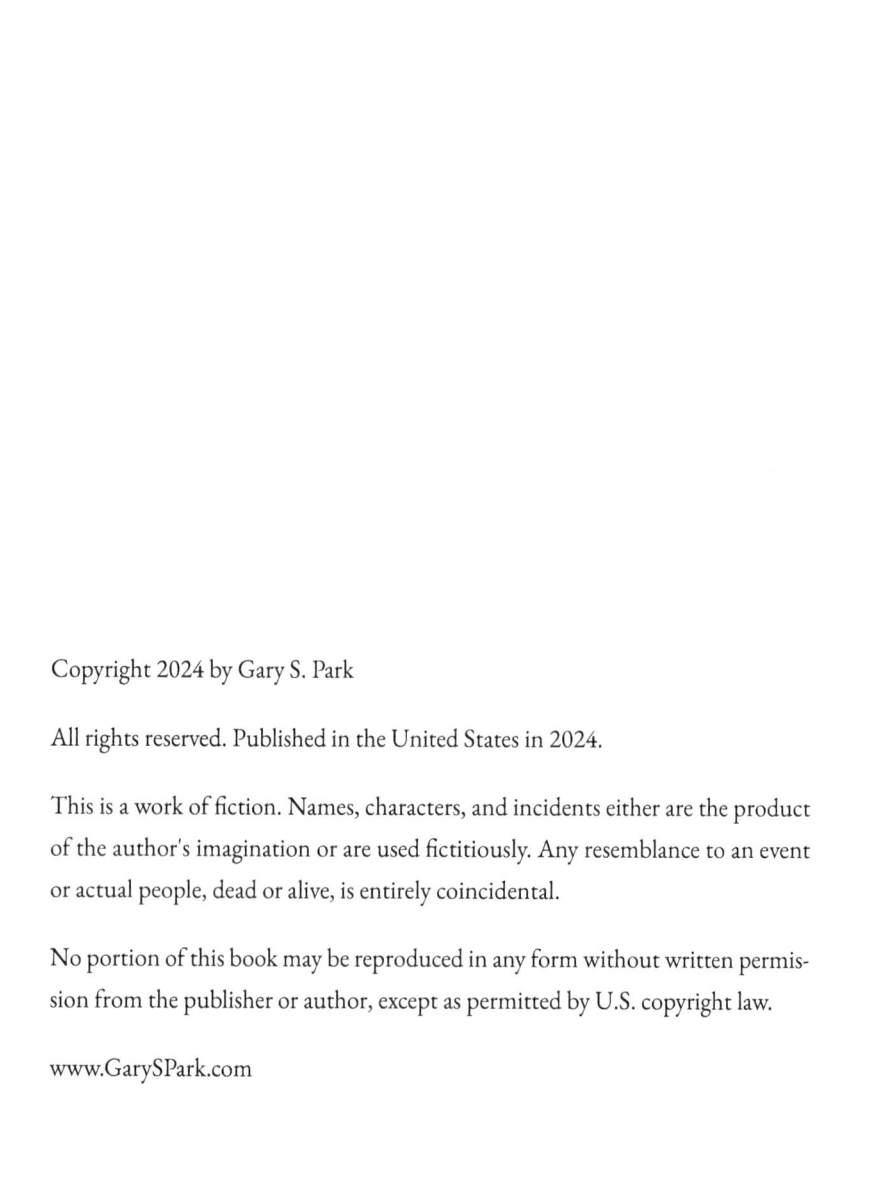

All rights reserved. Published in the United States in 2024.

This is a work of fiction. Names, characters, and incidents either are the product of the author's imagination or are used fictitiously. Any resemblance to an event or actual people, dead or alive, is entirely coincidental.

No portion of this book may be reproduced in any form without written permission from the publisher or author, except as permitted by U.S. copyright law.

www.GarySPark.com

To the brave souls who navigate the darkness of suffering and violence, seeking hope among despair. Your strength inspires the fight for justice and compassion in a world often shrouded in silence.

For the healers who stand at the crossroads of compassion and fury. To every person who has ever felt trapped between the desire for justice and the weight of the world.

And to the readers, thank you for joining Eliza on this journey of healing, vengeance, and self-discovery.

Your willingness to explore the shadows alongside her is a testament to the power of storytelling in illuminating the human experience.

In the fight against silence and suffering, your voices matter.

Don't be afraid to speak up.

Your own life might depend on it.

Contents

1. Chapter 1   1
2. Chapter 2   14
3. Chapter 3   24
4. Chapter 4   34
5. Chapter 5   50
6. Chapter 6   65
7. Chapter 7   73
8. Chapter 8   83
9. Chapter 9   101
10. Chapter 10   116
11. Chapter 11   131
12. Chapter 12   140
13. Chapter 13   150
14. Chapter 14   163

15.	Chapter 15	173
16.	Chapter 16	189
17.	Chapter 17	200
18.	Chapter 18	207
19.	Chapter 19	215
20.	Chapter 20	224
21.	Chapter 21	238
22.	Chapter 22	245
23.	Chapter 23	252
24.	Chapter 24	259
25.	Chapter 25	269
26.	Chapter 26	276
27.	Chapter 27	283
28.	Chapter 28	294

Chapter 1

You might expect a person like me to have some sort of backstory, perhaps stemming from a broken home or falling into the pitfalls of addiction. Read the biographies of multiple serial killers, and you'll find stories of abuse, single-parent families, alcoholism, drug dependence, and other common factors. Watch a few court sessions, and you'll likely hear the defense attorney trying to dismiss those as an excuse in an attempt to persuade the judge to show leniency while the prosecutor wants to bring down the hammer.

Would it surprise you to know that none of those issues pertain to me? Can you believe that when I started my career, I was completely unprepared for what was ahead? The truth is I had never been much of an outspoken person, usually the kind of woman you'd find sitting in the back, mingling with acquaintances here or there in an attempt to remain inconspicuous. It wasn't really shyness, per se, more of a preference for the observer side of life.

So what's Eliza Moore's typical nightlife? It consisted of a bowl full of cheese-flavored popcorn and watching a few episodes of Law and Order: SVU. I would often lose track of time, intrigued by the plot twists and suspenseful investigations. The captivating mysteries always made my day after working long hours at the hospital.

If you're curious, nursing wasn't always my life's ambition. When I was little, I actually wanted to work behind the scenes in movie productions. I desired to be a part of the best dramas and romantic comedies on the planet while making people laugh. That was the dream, but growing up, I realized it wasn't going to happen, not when you live in the nation's 66th most dangerous city. An individual strolling on the sidewalk faced a 1 in 40 likelihood of becoming a victim.

Instead, I felt called to become a nurse once I finished college and my two friends were heading off to med school. How is it possible for someone like me to transition from wanting to care for people to feeling the need to harm someone, you might ask? For that, I have to take you back...back to one specific evening in late October of 2021, a night when my eyes suddenly opened to a reality I had been suspicious of for a while.

Basin General Hospital not only holds some three-hundred-and-thirty beds but also a 24-hour Level 3 Trauma Center that could be considered one of the prime places to end up, given the demand on Friday and Saturday nights. The thirty-seven-bed, two-bay emergency department (ED) holds up pretty well most nights, but come the weekend, all bets are off. Overdoses, assaults, alcohol-related injuries, shootings, stabbings...they all go up exponentially through the weekend.

While the roster had me mainly working in the cardiac unit in the months leading up to that October night, I began to drift toward the ED more and more as demand called for it. I would often come in to start my shift in one unit, only to find that I had been reassigned due to staff shortages. Then, I'd spend the next twelve hours handling all sorts of nonsense to keep up with ever-increasing patients.

I loved it. Being given the chance to help people having the worst day of their lives is something you cannot understand unless you've experienced it for yourself. It wasn't just about saving lives. It was about helping those people through whatever trauma they experienced while making sure they came out the other end in one piece. The job offered a good variety of different situations, and I can honestly say that no two days were ever the same.

Friday and Saturday nights were when things got interesting; the night shift turned dark, almost on cue. Come six o'clock, the ODs began arriving as if scheduled. Next came the assaults, usually brought on by some barroom brawl involving the usual mix of testosterone, alcohol, and female influence. One after another, the injured arrived, either on foot or hand-delivered by law enforcement or the city's fleet of ambulances.

There was one specific night when you could say something in me changed. It's a date I'll never forget. Saturday, October 16th, 11:40 pm, to be precise. I started to realize that there was a distinct group of patients who would show up after a specific amount of time, and most people wouldn't have noticed the scenarios unless you interacted with them one-on-one.

This specific group of people usually walked in sometime after ten. You see, the typical instigator needed time to warm up and drink a few brews in order to get their temper just right. They needed to consume enough alcohol to prime their short fuse for the smallest of triggers that would ultimately send them into a rage. It was the same story set on repeat for us.

The most distressing aspect for me was that we had a name for it. We had to pinpoint and segregate these particular individuals in order to keep them apart from the others. We didn't say the words domestic violence. We kept it short enough to ensure that the actual phrase never saw the light of day in our department, with the entire staff referring to the matter as nothing more than a DV.

"Hey, Eliza, there's a DV waiting for you in Room 12," a colleague might say. Or "That DV in Room 4 needs cleaning up" and needs attention. I think, in a way, shortening the term down to just a couple of letters kind of numbed us to it.

DV wasn't a term I came to detest straightaway. In the beginning, it was just the lingo we used, a code we'd speak to maintain privacy. When working in the kind of hectic environment I was in, time mattered, even a second or two when sharing details with colleagues. But it wasn't long before those two letters began to irritate me for all the wrong reasons.

October 16th was the night when my life completely flipped for me. I had just finished cleaning up a young New Yorker who'd come to town for his friend's 21st birthday. And yes, by cleaning up, I mean the usual mix of blood and vomit that accompanied most late-night party people. This kid had the misfortune of losing his balance while standing on the edge of a porch and decided to fall on a bunch of cacti to cushion his fall.

"DV in Room 4, Eliza," was how Dr. Fitzby alerted me to my next job after the kid from New York. Usually, I wouldn't have thought much of it, simply washing my hands and moving on to the next patient in line. Not so this time.

To understand my apprehension, there's probably one other thing that you need to know about. Yeah, the ED housed thirty-seven rooms used for both assessing and treating new arrivals, but also five individual rooms that doctors used for a more private setting. These rooms were also used for the more... severe cases that needed to be kept out of the public's view. Needless to say, those who needed to be dealt with behind closed doors.

In essence, if a DV was taken to one of those rooms instead of our standard rooms, it can only signify one thing. They were messed up, in a really bad way. I could already feel my stomach tighten just after hearing the doctor's request. For these, I usually took a couple of deep breaths and jumped right in, but not this time. Even before opening the door, I knew this would be different.

Along with providing me with some instructions, Dr. Fitzby also handed me a clipboard holding the patient's admission slip. It gave me the basics such as name, age, condition, and stuff like that. I scanned over the information as I walked to the door and stopped when I spotted the name at the top of the page.

Neena Hurst was a name familiar to me. It took me a moment to recall the exact circumstances in which I became aware of it, but once I did, chills ran through me. She had been in the previous month, but not for herself. It had been for her 9-year-old daughter, Ally, who needed help with a broken wrist. At the time, I remembered being struck by how quiet the family was with Ally's younger sister, Grace, also in the room.

It was not unusual for families to be overwhelmed by shock, just like I believed Neena and her daughters had been. I remember seeing the fear in little Grace's eyes, fresh tears threatening to spill if she detected the slightest pain in her sister's eyes. Even Neena was scared, and her concern for her daughter was clearly written on her face.

Standing in the middle of the hall holding that clipboard brought the visit back and, with it, an uncomfortable question. Was the shock in the family's eyes from young Ally's injury really because of an accident? I stared at the sheet of paper with the doctor's words still ringing in my ears.

"DV," was what he said, a domestic violence case, and obviously alarming enough to require a private room.

More chills ran through me as I stared at the closed door and imagined the young family waiting for me behind it. Would it just be the mom this time? And if it was, where were her children? The PA suddenly clicked to life, a dozen or so speakers all waking up in unison as someone called for Dr. Fitzby to come to Station 1. The announcement gave me a kind of shove, and I continued, forcing myself not to stop until I opened that door.

When I reached for the handle, I took a couple of deep breaths, but I don't think it helped. My heart felt like a bass drum, the beating stretching all the way into my temples, but I knew I had to go inside. With a final sigh, I pushed the distracting thoughts aside and knew someone needed attention.

It was actually worse than I imagined. The tension hanging in the room felt thick enough to cut as I walked in. Neena sat on the edge of the bed alone, her face downcast as a man sitting in one of the chairs had his daughters balanced on each of his legs. The fear in their little faces eclipsed tenfold, just like what I'd seen during their previous visit, but more than that, I could see the shame in the young mom's eyes.

"Look, girls," the father said as he sat a little forward. "Here's the nurse to help mommy."

The stench of alcohol reached out to me as he spoke, a faint undertone of stale tobacco running alongside. He grinned up at me, the bloodshot eyes studying me as if wanting to say something else. I forced a grin and turned my attention to Neena, who looked like she'd gone ten rounds in a boxing match.

"Fell down the stairs, she did," Brian Hurst said as I looked into his wife's face. It was amazing how easily that lie rolled off his tongue. "If I haven't told her a thousand times to watch her step. Clumsy she is. Has been her whole life."

The busted lip was just the start of it, and the cut needed a couple of stitches to hold it together. From the depression I could see in her cheek, my guess was a fractured cheekbone.

One of her front teeth had gone AWOL, the other broken in half. Neena stared at me through her one good eye, the other almost entirely closed by a bruise continuing to bloom across her face. The dark purple hue seemed to be spreading aggressively, overshadowing her otherwise pale skin.

"I'll give you something for the pain," I said, speaking with a straightforward tone that I knew her husband would take offense to. Guys like him always did. The thought of a woman making decisions for herself always riled them up. I said, "It might be more comfortable for the girls to sit out in the waiting room while I help their mom, Mr. Hurst," as I stood there with my best posture.

"We're fine right here," he insisted.

Of course, he would say something like that.

What scared men like that the most was the possibility of their wives or partners being left alone and having the opportunity to share their experiences, disclosing the violence they had suffered to someone who could take action, such as myself. Men such as Brian Hurst were not fond of individuals like me. We threatened their way of life, and being left alone with their victims meant risk.

I could see they were beyond scared. Two little girls, much too young for the horror they had been forced to endure. I looked at Ally and wondered how the broken wrist really happened. As if sensing my curiosity, I watched Brian curl his arm around his daughter a little tighter while gazing at me. Our eyes met and it was apparent he knew what I was thinking.

"Will the doc be coming to help Neena, Nurse Moore?"

The door opened, and Dr. Fitzby walked in as if sent by fate itself, along with his X-ray technician. He ignored the husband entirely and gave the girls a quick wink before leaning down to the patient. Fitzby had walked these halls for more than a decade and knew the deal. He didn't need an explanation nor asked for one.

"Let's take a look at you," he said, trying his best to sound friendly with a forced smile, but I could see the same repulsion in him that I had.

Dr. Fitzby stood by the examination table, notifying Neena that she'd need an X-ray. The tech escorted Neena to the next room to stand in front of the radiographic grid and wrapped a radiation shield apron around her collar. After a few images were taken, the tech brought Neena back to her room while Dr. Fitzby took a look at the film.

The X-ray revealed a break in the zygomatic bone, commonly known as the cheekbone. Dr. Fitzby explained that the fracture had displaced the bone, which was why Neena was experiencing pain and bruising in the area. Surgery would be required right away to realign the bone and prevent long-term complications such as facial asymmetry or nerve damage.

In the operating room, the surgical team worked quickly. After placing Neena under general anesthesia, Dr. Simmons made a small incision near the site of the fracture. She used specialized instruments to delicately realign the displaced cheekbone. To secure and promote proper healing, a titanium plate and small screws were inserted to hold the bone in place. The surgery lasted about two hours, and everything went smoothly with no complications. Once the bone was secured and Dr. Simmons was satisfied with the alignment, the incision was closed with sutures.

Neena's recovery began in the hospital, where she was closely monitored for any signs of infection or swelling. For the first 24 hours, she was kept on pain medication and a soft food diet to minimize jaw movement. Swelling around her face was expected, but the medical staff reassured her that it would subside in a few days. After two days of observation, Neena was allowed to return home with instructions to avoid strenuous activities and to sleep with her head elevated to reduce swelling. Dr. Simmons scheduled a follow-up appointment a week later to check the healing progress, knowing that with proper care and rest, she was expected to make a full recovery.

We didn't bring up the alleged fall as the reason, and law enforcement wouldn't have anything without anyone talking. Neena ended up getting discharged from the hospital. She was sitting a little hunched forward while sitting in a wheelchair as she did her best to hide the damage to her face. There's nothing like flipping long hair over to cover the evidence. The trio was slightly ahead of Brian, who looked relieved to finally get out of there. He did give me a final up-and-down glance as he passed by my station, and this time, I didn't look away. I wanted him to know that I knew exactly what he was.

What I really wanted to do was report him to the authorities. It was because of the lack of intervention that usually kept these monsters out in the community to continue their terror. Victims like Neena, Ally, and countless others would continue to suffer if people didn't speak up. The hospital environment is about healing the sick and wounded. Dr. Fitzby and I had our hands tied, and eventually, Brian Hurst was out of our sight.

Neena Hurst wasn't the first victim of domestic violence I'd dealt with, not even close. She wasn't the first I wanted to help either. I think for me, it was all those patients who gradually made me frustrated with the system. The same system that allowed individuals like Dr. Fitzby to not necessarily ignore the issues but leave the hard work to someone else.

It was seeing the fear and the shame in those faces that continued to lead me to a point where I knew I could no longer stand back and ignore their unspoken cries for help. I might have drawn a line in the sand, so to speak, a tipping point where I could no longer turn a blind eye. I think Neena Hurst was the one who finally pushed me over it and forced me to act.

Chapter 2

When I say the Neena Hurst situation might have been the one to finally push me over the edge. It didn't happen immediately, or at least not in the sense you might expect. The interaction with Neena Hurst stayed with me throughout the rest of that day, and when I came in early for my shift two days later, I stopped by the room where she was assigned.

Heading to the locker room, renewed frustration grew inside me, the faces of those little girls staring out at me from the shadows of my mind. Not just theirs but also their very real memories of their mom; the damage to her face was just an indication of the kind of treatment she received behind closed doors. What Neena Hurst and her two young daughters needed was someone to stand up for them.

After dropping my gear into my locker and heading back out to the ED, I went looking for the only other person who dealt with the brutality that night. I found Dr. Fitzby sitting in the breakroom alone, one hand curled around a cup of coffee, the other holding the corner of a newspaper as his eyes ran across the print.

For a second, I just stood in the doorway, a little unsure of how to bring it up. He either hadn't heard me walk up or chose not to acknowledge me, continuing to read whatever article had caught his interest. Taking a deep breath, I pushed on, and when he flipped the page, Dr. Fitzby looked up, flashed me a grin, and continued reviewing the next page.

"I think we're in for a busy one, Eliza," he said with his polite British accent as I went to grab a drink of water. "Full moon out tonight," and then, under his breath, he added, "Always brings out the crazies."

"Let's hope not," I said and briefly turned my back as I filled a paper cup.

I took a drink but held the water in my mouth for a bit, the coolness reaching down as I pushed myself to speak up. The faces continued staring at me, almost guilting me into action. When I finally swallowed, I heard Fitzby turn another page and then another. Soon, he would grow tired of finding nothing else of interest, and he would excuse himself.

The newspaper was the only reason he ever came into this room. During my time working with him in the ED, it had become something of a running joke; the man was too cheap to buy his own newspaper. Of course, doctors had their own offices, and he could have read the paper in peace without constant interruption, but not Dr. Fitzby.

"Doctor, I need to ask you something, if I may," I said, finally turning back to face him. He looked up at me with that questioning expression of his, the one that always reminded me of some British monarch about to decide a peasant's fate. "It's about that young family from the other night."

"We see many families," he said. "Be more specific."

"Neena Hurst, the DV we treated, the mom with the two young daughters."

"Hurst, yes, of course."

"Shouldn't we be reporting it to the police?" I took a couple of steps forward and gripped the top of one of the chairs as I held my drink in the other hand. "I mean, it's our duty to report any suspected cases of domestic violence."

"Yes, I know the rules, Eliza. But unfortunately, when it comes to these types of incidents, there's very little we can do. If we reported every suspected case of abuse, we'd all end up spending countless hours as witnesses in court, leave this place grossly understaffed, and in nearly ninety-five percent of cases, the women almost always go back anyway."

"So, we do nothing?"

"Did you give this Hurst woman the pamphlets about domestic violence?"

"No, I couldn't. Every time I tried, the husband was there."

I could see from the look on his face that Neena Hurst and her daughters would never be a priority to him. Having spent the past twenty years watching people like the young mom walk through the doors had somehow numbed his sense of empathy. He didn't lack sympathy for them, but it was evident that he considered the struggle to help them as challenging or near pointless and eventually chose to ignore the issue.

Dr. Fitzby finished up his coffee, scrunched up his cup, and tossed it basketball-style into the trash. Next, he closed the newspaper, folded it in half, and placed it next to the napkin dispenser, ensuring the edge lined up alongside the metal container perfectly. He stood, looked at me for a second, and then turned to walk out. Just before he reached the door, he stopped to look back at me over his shoulder.

"Take it from me, Eliza. There will come a time when you will realize that the best thing you can do is treat their injuries and move on. People like Neena Hurst have to learn to fight their own battles and figure things out for themselves."

I stood there dumbfounded by his words. Fitzby didn't bother waiting for me to respond. He simply continued on with his afternoon as if he completely separated from the suffering surrounding us. His lack of empathy didn't just annoy me; it boiled my insides as I felt the heat of anger rising in my fists.

This man...no, not man...this arrogant cretin who wielded so much influence within the hospital didn't have enough compassion, leaving vulnerable people like Neena Hurst out to dry. I'm not sure how long I stood there grappling with my anger, but I didn't move again until one of the other nurses walked into the room.

Kristy said, "Eliza, hey," as she hurried to the fridge. Are you ready for another night?

"Yeah, sure," I said, as I sounded more than a little bit distracted, but thankfully, Kristy didn't notice.

"Had a crazy afternoon," she said before taking a massive bite of her sandwich.

"This kid on a skateboard broke his arm and nearly screamed the entire place down."

Bits of bread fell out as she spoke, but she barely noticed. Sometimes, swallowing food on the run was the only way for us to get sustenance during a shift.

"At least you get to go home soon," I said and headed out to begin my shift.

Fitzby had been right about one thing, though. That night turned out to be brutally busy. Not a lot of people believed it, but the myth about the full moon bringing out the crazies appeared true. Just ask any nurse working the night shift or even the other emergency services. I suppose law enforcement officers would encounter as much as we do. Despite all the distractions that night threw at me, it still wasn't enough for me to push Neena Hurst out of my mind.

Paramedics wheeled two car crash victims in around 2000 hrs. Then, there were four overdoses, three assault victims, half a dozen intoxicated injuries, and enough people suffering from illnesses to fill the waiting room out in the foyer. By midnight, the noises in the hospital reached concert level. Multiple drunks began to sing Irish songs at the top of their lungs to drown out a meth addict screaming for morphine to help ease the pain of an ingrown toenail.

Our feet were already tired, and I needed better shoes. We did the best we could, trying to calm everyone down. But all I kept thinking was finding Neena Hurst waiting in one of the rooms and what I would say to her.

And if you think that Neena Hurst's predicament only affected me while I was at work, you'd be sadly mistaken. She even invaded my thoughts while I sat home alone on my couch watching the television. It felt as if I'd been plagued by her memory, that battered and bruised face staring back at me with that ever-fearful look in her eyes.

One night, while sitting down with a microwaved dinner, I flicked on the television for a bit and settled on an old episode of I Love Lucy while looking through some social media. The food was slowly getting colder by the bite, which should have indicated the amount of time passing by. The shift from a 1950s sitcom to current events occurred after scrolling through some uploaded videos featuring a squirrel snatching a slice of pizza from a kitchen counter and a man attempting to take a flawless selfie with his dog only to end up getting his face licked.

After changing the channel to the news, I heard two attention-grabbing words that made the television screen the only thing I could focus on... domestic incident.

The footage the news reporter covered was a cuffed man being removed from a deputy's cruiser and led to the side entrance of the Ector County Sheriff's Office. The heavyset man kept his head lowered to avoid the cameras capturing a clear image of him, but it didn't matter when an earlier mugshot appeared on the top-right of the screen, showing his face.

I felt my heart sink when a photo of a young woman appeared in the very middle, her smiling face peering out from between long strands of blonde hair. The same helpless anger I'd felt when speaking with Fitzby in the lunchroom just a couple of days earlier flooded back when I heard the reporter update the anchor about the situation. The boyfriend with a long criminal history of violence and drug offenses had been out on bail for beating his former girlfriend. Unfortunately for his current girlfriend, the violence simply transferred to her and the mother of a young 3-year-old girl died from horrific injuries after a brutal beating.

The most sobering part for me came when the clip returned to where the reporter had set up outside the victim's home and I watched that young girl crying hysterically as someone carried her from the front door to a waiting car. So many lives destroyed in the blink of an eye, I thought to myself, and all because of some piece-of-shit lowlife with a bad attitude and complete disregard for anybody else.

I wanted to scream, my insides gripped by phantom fingers as that child's uncontrolled sobs joined the faces of Neena Hurst and her children in my mind. The victims appeared to congregate against me, forcing me to relive their fear and pain over and over again.

It may not have been the smartest move for me but after I muted the rest of the news, I opened a local news site on my cell phone and found the story halfway down the page. The victim's same photo I saw earlier on the television looked out at me from an online article where I found yet more information about a case I just couldn't ignore.

The woman's name was Robin Metzler, aged just twenty-four, and a mother to three-year-old Hazel. Originally from LA, Metzler moved to Odessa to be closer to her baby's father, but he died in suspicious circumstances the previous year. The more I read the story, the more I began to see an all-too-familiar theme of a single mom struggling with debt and isolation and opening up herself and her home to anybody willing to pay her some attention.

I couldn't help but shake my head; the story was just another one in a long line of people continuing to fall victim. What frustrated me more than anything was that I happened to be in a position where I could offer these victims help. My job alone should have been enough, and yet that was where I experienced the most resistance.

I think the other reason Robin Metzler sent me further down the rabbit hole of frustration at the system was the connection I felt with her. Having been raised by my grandmother after my mom passed away from cancer brought to light the little girl's future. In a way, I saw myself as little Hazel, a girl who would more than likely forget all the memories she had of her mother, a woman she would only ever know through photos and the stories shared by others.

I'm not sure how long I spent staring at that news story, but by the time I eventually shut my cell phone down, the closing credits to some Brad Pitt movie were already rolling. The thought of remaining on the sidelines while so many women faced such horror was probably my biggest struggle. Fitzby had made his position clear, and I knew that the rest of the system would side with him. If only I could find a way to help without compromising my own position or risking my job. The last thing I expected was for fate to step in as if answering my call for help.

Chapter 3

The month of November had almost come to an end when one significant event ensured the date would remain in the city's memories for years to come. On the night of the 28th, a multi-vehicle accident occurred out on the interstate, where it passed over the Grant Avenue intersection near the Holiday Inn. It was the hotel's parking lot where a lot of the emergency services set themselves up a base of operations to deal with the dozens of dead and injured.

We would eventually learn that the driver of a coach suffered a diabetic episode, his low blood glucose causing him to lose consciousness. The coach did manage to follow the Grant Avenue exit ramp but then careened directly into a second bus passing through the intersection. Two other vehicles somehow ended up entangled in the wreck, bringing the total number of people involved to fifty-seven.

Six people, including the diabetic driver, lost their lives in an instant, two more while en route to hospital. I wasn't scheduled to work that evening, but due to the scale of the emergency, management sent out a call for all staff, and I ended up racing to the ED to help out. I walked through the doors just after two that afternoon and wow, talk about an absolute madhouse.

Critical patients filled every operating theater, and we lined the overflow trolleys up along the walls of the hallways. I don't think there was a single staff member who didn't answer the call for help that day, and the pressure on us only got worse with each subsequent arrival. It was the first time I ever saw Fitzby appear completely out of his element, looking well but truly flustered as he tried to answer everyone's call for help.

It wasn't until almost six that things began to calm down enough for some of us to act as crowd control for the dozens still requiring help. I ended up sitting with an elderly woman named Doris Whitmore, who'd been brought in purely as a precaution after getting caught up in the accident while being a passenger in the cab. Fitzby gave her a quick once-over after being called to the woman by one of the nurses assigned to triage. He assigned her to one of the rooms for a bit of quiet observation time.

It was an error he would eventually come to regret in more ways than one.

When I wasn't called away for other random duties, Doris spent some time telling me all about her grandchildren, whom she was on her way to see. They were three young boys who had a passion for fishing at Calaveras Lake down near San Antonio. I could tell how much those boys meant to her by the way her face lit up each time she mentioned one of their names; her love was undeniable.

Just before seven, Lea Palmer called to ask if I could watch over her station for a few minutes while she took a bathroom break. After reassuring Doris that I wouldn't be long, I headed over to Station 2. I wasn't gone any more than ten minutes, and Lea even passed by Doris's room on her way back from the bathroom, but once I got returned to that sweet old lady, she'd already slipped away in silence. At first, I thought she'd just closed her eyes for a bit of rest. I know for me, the fluorescent lights can get a bit hard on the eyes and I've had plenty of patients place a blanket over their heads to get away from them.

Doris Whitmore wasn't sleeping, nor did she close her eyes because of the fluorescent lighting. The woman had died due to internal bleeding caused by the rear impact of the car accident that threw her into the cab's front seat. One of the arteries near her heart had ruptured just enough to cause a slow leak, and unfortunately, Fitzby failed to run her through the necessary checks. Doris showed no visible signs of physical distress nor complained of feeling lightheaded, so she was simply slid into the background.

It hit me hard finding her like that, but even harder after spending the next twenty minutes trying to revive her with Dr. Raj, another ED doctor. Doris ended up getting rushed into the closest surgery room, but every attempt made proved in vain. Fitzby, the dirty weasel, tried to push the blame on me, but Raj stepped in and put him back in his place.

Every single life we saved that afternoon fell by the wayside as my entire attention focused on the one that slipped through our fingers, the little old lady who sat quietly off to the side because she hated anybody fussing over her. She even told me so, asking if I could just put her in a cab and send her home where she would settle into bed with a nice cup of tea. According to Doris, there were other people who needed attention a whole lot more than she did. Both of us were utterly oblivious to the internal hemorrhaging.

Do you remember how I said that fate had a way of intervening when you least expect it? I think fate does a lot more than just intervene. Actually, I believe fate devotes a significant amount of time to carefully strategize how and when it will intervene in someone's life. Sometimes, a person affected by fate can trace the intervention back so many layers, to a point where it makes perfect sense that some kind of intelligence orchestrated the entire sequence of events.

If Des Hammond, the diabetic bus driver, had managed to purchase the soda he had brought to the counter at the previous gas station instead of finding his card declined, then maybe he would have managed to raise his blood glucose level enough for him not to pass out when he did. If the cab driver that Doris was riding with had not been preoccupied with scrolling through Instagram at the time of the collision, he might have been able to swerve and hit the brakes in time to avoid the impact. It would have prevented the frail old woman from being tossed around the vehicle.

If Alison Kemp's 29th birthday hadn't coincided with these events, Bella might not have proposed that we go out for a celebratory drink when the hospital finally discharged us just after ten that night. Unfortunately, all of those things did happen. That was how I ended up finding myself sitting at a table with three other nurses down at The Silver Lining Bar and Grill late that November night, wondering how the hell I ended up with a head full of bad memories and a weight of fatigue hanging heavy over me.

None of us were really in the mood to celebrate, not after watching so many people pass away from horrific injuries. The final death toll ended up being eleven, with twenty-eight remaining in hospital. Alison even apologized for dragging us down there. Of course, we all denied feeling that way, but I could tell she didn't believe any of us.

We did have a couple of drinks to celebrate, and when Naomi and Bella both called it quits after their second glass, we should have joined them. One thing was for certain, Alison wasn't convinced to leave quite yet, so we decided to hang back and unwind a little bit more. There was something I could see in her eyes that told me she wasn't quite ready to go home, so once the other two left, we ordered another drink for each of us.

Halfway through that third bourbon and coke, Alison began to open up about the trainwreck of a marriage she found herself in. She'd only been married to her high school sweetheart since the previous year, a wedding I had attended. They looked so in love that day, as Alison had every day since, which was why her revelation came as quite a surprise to me.

"I think Barry is cheating on me," she said when the first tears began to fall.

"Barry? Are you sure?"

I tried picturing her straight-laced nerd of a husband in the arms of someone else and couldn't. He just didn't seem like the kind of guy who could play on that field, not when his most exciting pastime involved sitting in front of his computer screen playing some war game.

"I heard him whispering to someone on his cell phone last week, and when I asked him about it, he acted all weird," Alison managed to whisper before the sobs took control.

Looking back, maybe it was that very sob session fate had also thrown into the mix to make sure I ended up exactly where it needed me to be. If it hadn't been for me leaning over and offering Ali my shoulder to lean on at that exact moment, who knows if I would have seen Brian Hurst standing near one of the far booths, trying to pull a strange girl closer to him. Alison really let go, maybe because of the alcohol in her system, and it gave me enough time to watch the married man try to force a kiss on the much younger girl who looked to be trying to pull herself free.

When Alison pulled back and dried her tears with a crumpled napkin, I tried to steal glances in Hurst's direction, but the seat backing blocked my view. I did slide a little closer to the edge a couple of minutes later, but by then, the domestic abuser had gone to where I didn't know.

We stayed for another twenty minutes or so, and once we finally left our booth, I scanned the room again but couldn't find Hurst or the girl he'd been trying to get with. I soon caught a glimpse of him getting into a beat-up junker in the parking lot. We had to head over to our car, which fortunately was at the other end of the lot; I had to concentrate on the present moment.

Not knowing the future, I previously offered Alison a ride to the bar after work, so I had to return her to the hospital parking lot. Who knows where I might have ended up if I didn't have to leave when I did, although I could have probably guessed. As Alison was sitting next to me, I chose to take the longer route out of the parking lot. We drove around another building and checked the lot from a distance, but Hurst had already left.

"Maybe I'll just take you home," I told Alison once I turned onto 2nd Street. I knew she wasn't exactly drunk, but she did have three drinks on a mostly empty stomach and had been quite emotional.

"No, honestly, I'm fine," she assured me when we pulled up next to her car, and after exchanging a cautionary glance between us, I gave in. Having had the same number of drinks, I couldn't exactly preach, could I?

I waited until Alison had climbed in and started her car, then slowly moved back enough to let her drive from the parking space. Once she pulled onto the road a few moments later, we each headed off in our respective directions. What I expected was for Doris to return to my mind as I navigated the dark streets, but she'd been pushed aside, by none other than Brian Hurst. The man not only brought back the memories of the night I first met him and his family but every bit of frustration as well. No, not frustration...anger. Red hot, uncontrollable rage. My fingers began cramping from me gripping the steering wheel as tightly as I was. The sound of a knuckle cracking broke the silence in the cabin.

Who knows how different things might have worked out if it hadn't been for a red light stopping me at the intersection of 4th and Grant. Those brief few seconds were enough to pause my trip home and send me in another direction entirely. Brian Hurst didn't just remain in my mind; his wife Neena also made her presence felt. I think my curiosity got the better of me, and when the light turned green, I took a right instead of a left and found myself driving toward a home I had no business even knowing.

OK, so I might have crossed the lines of my position when I memorized Neena's home address after that second hospital visit. At the time, it wasn't for any specific purpose other than curiosity and remembering repeat patients. It wasn't as if I immediately took a drive over there to check what sort of home they kept. However, I did pull up the residence on Google Maps and found the home on Streetview.

I drove with GPS directions and ten minutes later, found myself slowing down as I pulled next to the curb across the street from the Hurst's home. Just a single window appeared lit up, and the rest of the house was sitting in darkness. The junker I'd seen earlier that night sat in the driveway, right behind the typical suburban family SUV.

Maybe my curiosity just refused to quit, so I decided to sit there and wait. I rolled down my window and killed the engine. Some random dogs barked a few streets over, and I heard a few vehicles cruising along I20, but the neighborhood itself remained silent. I think I just wanted to listen to the house itself, to see whether Hurst came home drunk and beat up his wife again. Maybe the guilt of seeing him in the bar and keeping it to myself was what brought me to the home. Either that, or I just felt a kind of protective urge for the mother and daughter I knew to be inside the house. Maybe it was the thought of them suffering through another night of abuse that brought me there.

I must have sat there for more than an hour just watching the house and trying to listen for any hint of shouting, but nothing happened. The light glowing in that small room remained on, and I figured it must have been some kind of nightlight, maybe one Neena set up for her daughters. In any case, when I still hadn't heard anything coming from the house by 1, I decided that it was probably best I headed home. Little did I know that it wouldn't be the last time I found myself sitting across the street from that house in the late hours of the night.

Chapter 4

Despite not being scheduled on the following day, I did end up with an afternoon shift after Alison called in sick. She'd sent me a message first, of course, just to see whether I'd be OK covering for her. What are friends for, was what I messaged back to her, although I did make sure she was alright, especially after her mini breakdown the previous night. She reassured me that all was well, explaining it was merely a brief emotional moment and that she was feeling much better now.

The shift itself turned out to be one of the better ones I'd had in recent weeks. Yes, we ended up getting run off our feet but we were busy in a good kind of way, if that makes sense. I didn't mind being busy as long as it didn't involve walking around listening to endless drunks demanding attention or puking all over the place.

For me, that shift turned out to be one of the better ones after so many crap ones. I actually sent Alison a text halfway through, first double-checking on her to see if she was still OK and then thanking her for giving me some more hours. Good shifts were a rarity in our profession, and so when we had the chance to work one, we truly learned to value it.

The problem was that I couldn't stop thinking about the night before. It wasn't just the hour or so I spent watching the Hurst house like some crazed stalker sitting in the shadows, but more so seeing Brian in that bar and sleazing himself around the place. What I couldn't get out of my mind was the unseen image of Neena lying all alone in her bedroom while her husband was out betraying the marital vows he obviously didn't cherish.

Did she know? That was a question I kept asking myself. Did the young mom of two little girls know that while she tried her best to keep a typical family home, her husband and the father of her children was out drinking and trying to hook up with anybody willing to pay him attention? Those thoughts kept me distracted during my downtime, somehow making the time pass even more quickly for me.

When I finished my shift around ten that evening, what I envisioned doing was heading home for a nice soak in a hot bath and the latest James Patterson thriller. If I had only listened to my inner voice warning me not to abandon my plans for the sake of quenching my overbearing curiosity. I heard a couple of the other nurses talking about needing a drink after a long shift and found myself standing on the very edge of a precipice I knew would essentially affect my entire future.

Standing in front of my locker, two nurses stood at the other end of the row and probably didn't even notice me there. Facing away from them, I could feel the weight of the moment as time seemed to slow down. If I turned around and made eye contact with them, they would no doubt ask me to join them. Since our group always went to the same place, it was almost a given that I could give in to my curiosity about whether or not Brian Hurst would again be strolling the bar looking for an all-new conquest.

Peg closed her locker, the metal door clanking into place as I stood my ground.

Just don't move, my inner voice told me for the second time.

Don't move, and you'll be relaxing in a nice hot bubble bath within the hour.

I could feel fate tapping me on the shoulder, almost trying to entice me to follow the other choice waiting for me. I closed my eyes, listening as the second locker door slammed shut, and finally made my decision.

"Hey, Liz," Peg called out when I turned to face them and shot off a smile. "Wanna come out for a quick drink with us?"

"Sure, I could go for one," I said as I closed my own locker, the slamming door sounding more like me sealing my fate.

Twenty minutes later, the three of us sat in the very same booth I had been in the previous night, each sipping a white wine and talking about a vacation Mackenzie was planning for the following year. I listened to her with a hint of jealousy. Scotland is one of those countries I've wanted to travel to for years. She was beginning to talk about an Air BnB she and her partner had booked themselves right on Loch Ness when a loud and obnoxious laugh suddenly interrupted her. We all turned to see, and that was when I first spotted Brian Hurst back doing what he seemed to do best.

The married father of two stood near the end of the bar with a glass of beer in one hand and his other on the shoulder of a woman who didn't look overly enthused by his advances. He kept leaning in to try to whisper something into her ear, but the woman repeatedly turned her head away. Her friend, sitting on the other side of her, could be seen asking him to leave them alone, and she eventually looked around for the bartender.

"What a creep," Mackenzie said as she turned back to us and continued sharing more details of her trip, but I was barely able to listen anymore. All my attention was riveted on the man who should have been at home, tending to the needs of his family. Instead, he stood there, oblivious to the chaos he was creating around him. I couldn't help but feel a mix of anger and disbelief as I watched him flirt so shamelessly, seemingly indifferent to the responsibilities he'd abandoned. With each laugh and every failed attempt to charm the women nearby, I grew more unsettled, grappling with the stark contrast between his carefree demeanor and the heavy burden of family life that he was neglecting. It was as if he was living in a different world, one where duty and love no longer held any sway over his actions.

The bartender eventually appeared and called for Hurst to leave the two women alone, and while he did comply, it wasn't long before he turned his attention to another group sitting in one of the booths further up from us. I could still see him from my vantage point, watching the man half stagger as he tried engaging with the two women.

It was Peg who finished her drink first and said she needed to get home. Mackenzie finished the rest of her wine and followed suit, but I wasn't ready. Maybe if I had, this story would have taken yet another turn and not gone down the path I would eventually find myself on. Unfortunately for me, my bladder had other ideas.

"You guys go ahead," I said. "I'm just going to the restroom."

"Want us to wait?" I looked at Peg and smiled.

"No, seriously, I'm a big girl," I said. "You're both on tomorrow, right?" They both nodded. "I'll see you at work."

I finished the rest of my drink and as we stood, I gave each of them a hug before turning to the hallway leading down to the restrooms. Aside from the two doors leading into each gender's bathroom, there was a third door for the back of the bar, a fourth for an office, and one at the very end, I assumed leading out onto the loading dock. The green Exit sign flickered as I stole a glance at it before I pushed open the door into the ladies room.

The three tiny stalls all stood empty as I entered, and aside from the smell of stale urine, the facilities weren't too bad. I'd been in worse ones, and just having doors on the stalls gave these a substantial advantage over some of the worst. I went to the far left one and did my business in silence as I listened to the muffled sounds of the distant bar. I could hear some of the voices but not what was being said or by who. I imagined going back out and finding the girls waiting for me, so I didn't want to keep them waiting too long.

I did check my reflection in the mirror when I washed my hands and sighed at the face staring back at me. It didn't feel like my own, the long days and nights working under the constant stream of fluorescent lights seeming to sap the very life from my skin. It was either that or just the stress of the job wearing me down. In any case, it saddened me to think that doing something for the greater good was actually hurting me in some way, as if penalizing me for my contribution to society. Is that really how it was supposed to play out?

I was still running that question through my head when I stepped out of the bathroom and into the hall again.

"I knew I recognized you," a voice suddenly said from behind me and I spun around so fast, I nearly tripped over my feet.

Hurst took a step toward me and grinned wide enough for his teeth to show, his bloodshot eyes focused on me. "Yeah, I do. You're that nurse from the hospital, ain't ya?"

"What do you want," I said, feeling instant repulsion. Rather than answer, he stopped and leaned back slightly as his eyes slowly worked their way down the length of my body before coming back up to meet my own.

"To see where those legs come together," he crooned, taking another step closer.

"You're disgusting," I said and took a step back. "Shouldn't you be home with your wife?"

"I bet you could do a lot more than she ever has," he said. "How about it?"

I couldn't help it, the laugh slipping out of me before I had a chance to reel it back in. It seemed to hit Hurst in just the right spot, the man suddenly looking wounded by the sound of it. For a man who liked to beat women, I was surprised when he shook his head and walked away from me, eventually disappearing through the last door with the Exit sign hanging over it. I thought I heard him mutter the word bitch under his breath as he pushed the door open, but I couldn't be sure.

I'm not sure what emotion kept me standing there more, the curiosity of why the man had left the building via the back door or the anger I felt slowly building inside me again. Maybe it was a combination of the two, or perhaps even just the fact that Hurst managed to get in the final word, another insult thrown at the women of the world.

In any case, I found myself unable to turn back to the bar and walk away; the urge to finally let him know exactly how I felt was impossible to ignore. I did take a look back behind me toward the bar, but it wasn't enough to change my mind. Walking with purpose, I walked to the door, pushed it open, and sealed my fate.

At first, I couldn't make sense of what I found on the other side. Another much shorter and much darker corridor met me; the floor turned from floorboards to concrete. It turned a 90-degree corner and when I reached the bend, I not only found the actual loading dock but also Brian Hurst standing on the edge of it urinating. He stood to one side, so he wasn't exactly facing away from me, which was why he must have spotted me the second I stepped around the corner.

"I didn't expect you to take up my offer," he said hungrily and to make his point, he turned slightly around and showed me himself.

If it hadn't been for the anger continuing to build up inside me, I might have taken that as the cue to get the hell out of there. But the truth is, I was already in a bad spot at the wrong time. The vision of Neena Hurst's battered face looking back at me from the seat in the examination room proved too much for me to ignore.

"What sort of a man goes out night after night hitting on women while his wife and children wait for him back at home," I said as I slowly walked toward him.

"Physical Abuse, there's the phrase of the year, isn't it?

It must feel so empowering to beat up a helpless woman. What is it? Don't you have any real friends, so you feel the urge to make the little woman pay for your... shortcomings?"

"What?" He sounded more shocked than surprised, but I wasn't about to stop.

"What a tough guy you are." I continued to advance on him but really had no clue what I was going to do once I reached him.

"No really, super tough beating up someone who gave you two children and will do anything to protect her family. Must be so-"

"You shut the hell up," he suddenly snapped as he tried to zip up.

"Shut your mouth, or I'll-"

"You'll what," I said. "Hit me?" Now, it was my turn to chuckle.

"Guess you're used to that, aren't you? Beating up women? Only I'm not going to let you get away with it. No, I'm going to make sure everybody knows who you are and what you like to do. Just wait until the press hears about you."

The anger had quickly turned to rage, and I lost all perception of the danger I was in. Hurst, finally managing to zip up his pants, he lunged forward and grabbed for me. I tried to deflect him, but he got a good hold of my wrist.

"I'll shut you up myself," he said as he pulled me close enough to smell the rank tobacco on his breath. He spun me around, wrapped one arm around my neck, and pulled me close to his chest.

That was when I realized the error of my ways. The panic set in as Hurst tried to pull me away from the help beyond the door. I did my best to break myself free, but despite the alcohol in his system, the man still had enough strength to overpower my efforts. When I tried to scream, his arm tightened enough to cut off my air supply, and that was when the real hysteria set in. This was the kind of drunken situation where people died, and I imagined Hurst later weeping to some cop that he never meant to kill me.

Feeling the life slipping away from me, I did the only thing I could think of, one last attempt to free myself. I lifted my legs to curl my body into a ball to let Hurst take my full weight, something I felt to be impossible given the position of his arms. He lost his grip on me, and I began to fall, but I managed to get my feet back on the ground just in time. If he had completely let go of me at that point, things might have turned out differently, but unfortunately, he didn't and tried to get a hold of me again. Our feet became entangled as his hands tried to find something to hang onto. I shook him off really hard, and he lost his balance, let go, and gravity took over.

The sudden shift in weight caused Hurst to not only stumble backward, but his arms began to cartwheel crazily as he tried to catch himself. He barely managed more than a couple of steps before the ground beneath him ran out. I hit the ground hard and spun around to save myself from any possible follow-up attack but lost sight of Hurst as he fell off the loading dock. He shrieked during his plunge, but the sound cut off a split second later as he hit the ground, the impact silencing him in an instant.

For the first brief moment, I barely moved; the throbbing in my arm and the shooting pain in my knee held my attention. I ran one hand down my leg while checking my neck, feeling for blood, but I couldn't detect any. That was when I realized I still hadn't heard anything from the fallen drunk still lying somewhere out of sight. Pushing myself off the ground, I rose to my feet and took a couple of steps toward the edge. The street light 50 feet away at the edge of the property wasn't strong enough to light up the area, but I could see enough to know that the fall had rendered my attacker unconscious.

Being a nurse, my first instinct forced my feet to move, and I climbed down the steps, heading down one side of the dock to check on the man. There wasn't enough light for me to see his face, but I did press a couple of fingers on the side of his neck to check for a pulse as I kneeled beside him. I assumed I'd feel his heartbeat and was already preparing my other hand to feel for any blood on the back of his head when I felt a chill run through me...no pulse.

Panic set in almost immediately, the kind that usually led to poor judgment, the kind read out in court by a defense lawyer trying to justify his client's stupid actions. In other words, the type that didn't lead to smart decisions. I held my breath as I leaned down, straining to hear a breath that I knew wouldn't come.

"Son of a bitch," I muttered under my breath, suddenly all too aware of the precarious situation I'd managed to put myself in. Fearing the worst, I pulled out my cell phone, activated the flashlight, and froze as I stared into the lifeless eyes of Brian Hurst, a man whose wife-beating days had finally come to a sharp and sudden end.

A thousand thoughts hit me all at once in conjunction with a boatload of adrenalin. I felt my insides just about to turn inside out as the light from my cell phone began to shake uncontrollably.

"No," I whispered, the panic robbing me of the last remaining bit of common sense.

It was obvious he was dead, and there was no coming back. The glazed-over eyes stared back at me as if announcing his departure; the soul flung out at the moment of impact. My guess was some sort of brain aneurysm or perhaps even a snapped neck. I immediately pulled my fingers back. My reflex action was so fast that I lost my balance and tumbled into the wall behind me.

The situation was simple. Before me lays a dead man who attacked me and somehow ended up losing his footing and fell to his death. I could picture a hungry prosecutor telling a jury about a nurse who knew him from the hospital where his abused wife had sought treatment. A woman who came to a bar two nights in a row where the deceased had been drinking. Ensured they would somehow meet in the back loading dock and then kill him by pushing him off the edge.

I could even hear the prosecutor's voice in my mind.

More panic set in. I had to get out of there. No amount of medical aid would help Hurst anyway. If I ran back into the bar, too many questions would arise, and then all of the focus would fall on me.

Not him...not the man responsible for beating his wife and children.

God knows how many times...

Not all the women he had already tried to prey on during his drunken sessions.

No, not them...me.

I would be the one to have to answer all the questions.

I stood upright and switched off the flashlight. Looking behind me and all around, I thought about the people in the bar and the possible questions they would throw at me. And that was when the other two faces came back to me.

"Oh, shit. Peg and Mackenzie." Would they still be waiting for me in the bar?

Before I had a chance to fully consider my options, I found myself already walking away, climbing the half-a-dozen steps back up to the loading dock and heading for the door. I paused again briefly when I reached out for the door handle, and then I felt my other hand suddenly pull the sleeve of my cardigan over my hand before grabbing the handle.

Just knowing I had taken steps to try and hide any evidence of me being back there sent a fresh surge of panic through me. I almost turned around to try and find another way out of there but knew I had to go back inside. If I didn't return and my two friends were still in the bar waiting for me, then that would almost guarantee more questions.

I opened the door as nonchalantly as possible, and when I saw nobody standing in the corridor, I made sure to wipe any possible fingerprints from the inside door handle as well. When I reached the corner, I stopped and took a prolonged and calculated look around the edge but again found the corridor empty. This time, I hurried, adding some extra speed to my step as I passed by the Ladies' bathroom door. Just before I walked back into the bar area, I took a deep breath, forced a casual smile, and headed in.

Not only were my fellow colleagues not at the table, but the bartender wasn't anywhere to be seen. The three people seated at the bar were all watching some prerecorded ballgame on the television. A couple was snuggled in a booth, their arms wrapped tightly around one another as they shared a passionate kiss.

Taking advantage of the opportunity, I didn't bother hanging around. The second I realized nobody was going to miss me, I headed to the door and walked out into the night. Neither Peg's Golf nor Mackenzie's Corolla remained in the parking lot, and for once, I was happy they actually took my advice to head home without waiting for me. It wasn't until I reached my Civic and climbed into the driver's side that I began to breathe a little easier. That was until I spotted something ominous hanging from the corner of the building, something that immediately sent a fresh wave of panic through me.

The security camera I first spotted looked to be pointing directly at the front door while a second nearby camera sat aimed down the side of the building. My heart dropped all the way down as I could barely suck in enough air, the sudden realization of another camera watching the loading dock almost a guarantee. I considered climbing out of the car and walking around the outside perimeter to check, but then I realized it wouldn't change a thing. If it had captured the entire event, then my goose was already well and truly cooked.

Chapter 5

Don't even ask me about sleep that night. Not only didn't I bother with going to bed, but I also spent every waking hour on my laptop trying to figure out whether the security system at The Silver Lining Bar had a camera around the back courtesy of Google Maps. Not only that, but I also repeatedly scrolled through every possible news site and social media platform I could, looking for any news about the dead guy I knew to be lying around the back of a particular bar.

If it hadn't been for my midday start time at the hospital, who knows how long I would have sat on my couch with multiple electronic devices at my fingertips? I didn't get ready until after ten and had to rush through my shower to make sure I would make it to work on time. As I was making my way to the hospital, my curiosity started to take over. I couldn't resist taking a slight detour to catch a glimpse of The Silver Lining, even if it was just a quick drive-by.

What I expected to find were multiple police cars and ambulances lined up across the parking lot, perhaps a few officers monitoring the roads for anybody looking suspicious. Instead, I found the place looking every bit as normally expected, the parking lot holding just about the usual number of vehicles and no sign of law enforcement. To ease my curiosity even further, I also turned down a side street, drove about halfway down the road, and turned around before scanning the rear of the premises for a dreaded security camera.

I made it almost back to the corner before my heart sank yet again as I spotted a long, rectangular hunk of metal hanging off the rear of the building and pointing directly down at the loading dock. What I couldn't understand was why the police hadn't yet been called on me if someone had spotted my interaction with the dead guy.

"Maybe they haven't found him yet," I thought to myself as I slowed near the driveway leading to the gates near the loading dock. It appeared locked, a thick chain supporting a substantial padlock that hung between the gates, and neither the gap under them nor between them looked wide enough for anyone to squeeze through.

There were so many unknowns. I took my foot off the brake and accelerated away. It was answers I came looking for, and yet I ended up leaving with more questions, like why it appeared as if the authorities hadn't yet been notified of the death. That was when it hit me, the answer was more than evident if I'd bothered to slow my over-assumptive brain down enough to think logically.

"He wasn't dead," were the words that rolled from my lips as I turned onto Grant Avenue.

It was the only answer that seemed to make sense to me. The only one that potentially fits the rest of the circumstances. Hurst must have knocked himself out when he fell, and maybe his eyes hadn't been opened quite as far as I had assumed. It had been dark, after all, and I had been quite tired. Who knew how much the wine had affected me? And then, there was the adrenalin from him grabbing me, the situation more frightening when he tried to choke me.

Thinking I'd cracked the puzzle, I looked at my watch as I considered doing a quick drive-by of Hurst's home. Maybe he'd gone home to sleep things off after managing to get himself out of the loading dock area. I could almost picture him climbing the steps while rubbing the back of his head.

"Not enough time," I said as I saw that I had just ten minutes to get to work, barely enough to drive to the hospital, park the car, clock in, get to the staffroom, and stow my gear.

Once I'd made up my mind to drive past the Hurst home after work, I felt a little better. Sure, the shift would be a long one, thanks to my brain continuing to badger me about all the possibilities, but I felt pretty good about my explanation of things that more than likely played out. As long as Hurst was alive, then there really wasn't anything for me to worry about.

When I walked into the staffroom, with just a couple of minutes to go before my shift, I found Peg standing near the soda machine talking with one of the other nurses, a new trainee named Elouise. She waved at me as I walked past on my way to the lockers.

"Hey, did you make it home OK last night? Kenzie had to rush home and didn't want to walk to her car alone."

"Nah, I was good," I said, more than aware that it was the first official lie I'd ever told a colleague of mine.

After dropping my handbag into my locker, I headed back to the soda machine and introduced myself to the trainee who happened to be starting on my very shift. Peg had already gotten turnover from the previous shift, so all I had to do was figure out which patients were mine on our way back to the station. According to my colleague, this morning had been fairly busy, but none of the patients really stood out. It was the usual bunch of small-town emergencies for a weekday morning.

"They did have a double overdose around four this morning," Peg said as we looked over the patient board. I gave a quick wave to a couple of others.

"Guy and his girlfriend both passed out right in the middle of 7th and Golder. A passing patrol car found 'em and called it in."

"Are they OK?" Peg rolled her eyes.

"Both are up in the unit. Guy got mighty pissed when we woke him up and ruined his high."

"Did you tell him that this situation could have had an alternative outcome?"

"Do they ever care?"

She was right, of course. It wasn't uncommon for paramedics to face some serious assaults because they were trying to save addicts from potentially fatal overdoses. I've seen more than my fair share of injuries during my time.

We spent about another twenty minutes going over the current patients awaiting assessments within the ED before I began my afternoon. Elouise remained by my side for all of the first hour until Fitzby called her away to follow him around. He was the kind who loved the attention, especially when it came from fresh-faced trainees swooning over anybody with a stethoscope and a BMW.

The first couple of hours proved to be the quietest of the shift as we helped just a dozen or so patients up until 1500 hours. I helped stitch a deep cut on a young butcher's thumb, as well as set a broken wrist for a seven-year-old. We also had an asthma attack, a couple of sprained ankles, and a fainting spell. The rest were the usual bunch of headaches, upset stomachs, and an irregular heartbeat.

My mind kept drifting back to the loading dock from the previous night each time I let my concentration run free, and to be honest, I could sense the panic waiting for me just beneath the surface like a hungry predator waiting to pounce. I knew that if I gave in to the unanswered questions, then it would potentially open a Pandora's Box of misinformation that I would struggle to contain again.

While not so for the patients who began arriving, I did find the afternoon rush to be almost a blessing in disguise for me. Not only did I completely forget about my concerns, but Fitzby also returned Elouise Carter, and she accompanied me through a few hours of assessments and subsequent treatments where necessary. The rest of the shift virtually flew by as we dived into our work and treated some sick patients.

It wasn't until the very moment I climbed back into my car just before nine that evening that the Brian Hurst dilemma came flooding back, and I once again faced my own inner demons as they demanded answers I didn't know If I would ever find. The first thing I did once the engine was running was to turn on the radio and tune into the local news channel. I was already out of the parking lot, and out on the road when the latest report came to air, but again, frustration set in when nothing about a body found at The Silver Lining made the headlines.

I knew I needed to find answers right then and there. The last thing I could see was me making it through another night, continuously trying to find answers to the dozens of questions rolling around my brain. It was almost a comical feeling as my body took over as it somehow turned on autopilot. I found myself being driven toward the Hurst household. Just as I had the first time I'd come to the street, I slowed well before the house and eventually pulled in close to the gutter to give myself time to check things out.

Imagine my relief when I spotted the junker parked by the house, not in the driveway like the last time but more on the grass and a little closer to the fence. The house itself appeared more lit up, but with all of the blinds drawn, it made sneaking a look inside near impossible. Rather than winding the windows down and shutting off the engine, I decided that seeing the car was enough proof for me to continue with my life. It appeared as if Brian Hurst had managed to make it home after all, and that was good enough for me.

Feeling a lot better about the situation, for whatever that's worth, I returned home. After walking into my apartment, I ended up opting for that long-awaited bubble bath I'd been promising myself. With enough bubbles both in the tub and in the glass I'd poured myself, I spent almost an entire hour with my face hidden underneath a wet towel. The darkness felt practically as soothing as the heat from the water itself, the shadows proving to be a welcome distraction from the stroke-inducing stress of the previous twenty-four hours.

What I did notice when I eventually fell into bed that night was the fact I hadn't eaten a single thing the entire day, nor was I hungry for anything. Instead, I barely kept my eyes open long enough to secure the house, switch everything off except the small lamp next to my bed, and then make sure the alarm for the following morning was switched off. I truly believed I had earned myself a sleep-in and that was precisely what I intended to do.

Despite having my questions answered and my mind eased by finding the junker home where it belonged, my subconscious still managed to prolong the suffering by delivering one hell of a nightmare for me to endure. I distinctly remember waking up twice throughout the night, each time finding myself dripping with sweat while feeling the aftereffects of a scream in my throat. I even got out of bed to grab myself a drink of water before climbing back in for a subsequent installment of the dream.

When a bloodcurdling scream woke me the following morning, I again found myself dripping with sweat, the bedsheet wrapped tightly around my legs as my eyes struggled against the blinding sunlight pouring in through the open window. Flashes of the nightmare were already fragmenting before fading out completely, and what I was left with was this stupid fear hanging over me as I held a hand up to shield my face from the sun. I'd forgotten to draw the blinds down after my fatigued late-night bath.

What did bring a smile to my face was the realization that I had the entire day to myself. Actually, I had two days off, and I wasn't about to waste them on unnecessary distractions the way I had the previous couple. I checked the time, saw that it was just shy of eight o'clock, and grinned. Once I remembered my plans, I actually jumped out of bed with an extra spring in my step. First, I took care of my bathroom needs, and after a quick, coolish shower to wash away the sweaty nightmare residue, I made myself a nice hot black coffee and took it to the couch for a bit of normality.

Nothing felt more normal to me than a cup of coffee and the morning news. While I knew most people preferred scrolling through whatever social media platform they happened to be on, I still hung onto a little bit of tradition. My grandma used to insist on nothing but coffee and her newspaper each morning, delivered to her front door by our neighbor, Frank. An early riser, Frank used to head down to the local store at six every morning and pick up two copies of whatever newspaper he fancied. He would drop one off for my grandmother; what a nice guy.

After making myself comfortable, I thumbed the screen of my cell phone, opened the Chrome app, hit the bookmarks tab, and clicked on the first of my saved news sites...CNN. I liked reading about international and national issues first. It was better to know what was going on in the greater world first to understand if anything significant would impact my life. It looked like a fairly standard sort of news day from first look. I found a story about climate change and economics, some political articles that I really didn't feel like getting involved with, as well as an article about a humpback whale getting caught in some nets off the coast of Australia.

I chose the whale story for a bit of light reading while taking a few sips of coffee, each time feeling the bitterness warm up my insides on its way down into my stomach. Coffee really was the best start to the day, and with the added sunshine, I knew this was going to be a great day. Throw in a trip to the mall for some late Fall bargains and a bit of shoe shopping later that afternoon, and who knew where else it would lead?

Half a cup was what it took me to get through several news sites before I switched tempo and went for a bit of social media scrolling. Instagram first, followed by a few scrolls through Facebook. I wasn't actually much interested in the latter but used it to get through the rest of my coffee. Two minutes later, and that's when I saw the post that would ultimately change the course of my day...my week...my entire life.

It was the photo someone had posted that drew my attention. The picture looked like the result of one of those studio deals that are sometimes offered to lure customers in before throwing photo packages worth hundreds of dollars to cover the walls of your house. The recognized family photo appeared happy, with two young girls sitting in the laps of each of their parents. The day must have been memorable for the mom, the smile appearing a lot more genuine than the one she tried to offer me while I was attending to her injuries. Even Brian Hurst looked to be thrilled at the chance to pose with his family, one arm around the shoulder of his wife, the other held around his youngest daughter's middle.

My eyes drifted down to the post's headline as the first bit of tightness nudged my insides, phantom fingers working themselves around my stomach. When I saw the very first capitalized word, those fingers began to squeeze, instantly pulling me back into the darkness of despair.

GoFundMe - Your friend Alison Kemp has already donated to this cause.

Will you be the next to help this worthy cause?

I wanted to click the link, but my fingers began to shake uncontrollably, and I only managed the edge of the Donate button, instead watching my finger hit the Comments section. In an instant, dozens of random people filled my feed with multiple comments about the unpredictability of life and how a person never knew how long they had left.

"What the," I faintly heard in the silence of the room as an uncomfortable beating began focusing in the middle of my chest. Halfway down the screen was where the first real indication jumped out at me with a random comment made by someone calling themselves Trent_Gunner942.

I hope he didn't land in his own piss, was the comment, and judging by the number of angry-face emojis linked to the text, I could tell it wasn't a well-taken comment.

Beads of sweat began to break out across my brow as I closed the comment section, and this time, clicked the Donate button. The screen briefly went black before the same family photo appeared at the top half of the page while black text filled the white bottom section. My eyes began to scan through the passage, my heart sinking further with each word.

I read the information twice, just to be sure, and still found myself unable to believe it. Knowing how rampant online scams were, I shut down the social media feed and opened a new Chrome page to try and confirm the story for myself. The first three local news sites had nothing, making no mention of the supposed tragedy. Feeling my desperation grow, I searched for one of the smaller independent sites I'd begun following the previous year, one of those lone-reporter-type

Instagram accounts. Seven posts down and I felt my entire world fall to the floor.

Tragedy struck the heart of Odessa late last night when 38-year-old Brian Hurst fell to his death after an accidental fall behind the popular The Silver Lining Bar and Grill. Patrons noted the man's intoxicated state at the time of his suspected fall. Mr. Hurst wasn't found until the following morning during an early delivery to the bar.

Authorities have yet to release an official statement, but an unnamed source confirmed that the married father of two appeared to have walked out onto the bar's loading dock to relieve himself but lost his footing before falling heavily to the ground. An autopsy report is being prepared by the coroner and should be available in the coming days. As always, I'll keep you guys updated as news comes to hand. It is believed that the man did not have any life insurance and friends have set up a GoFundMe page to help out in these tragic circumstances. I've copied the link below for anybody interested.

I couldn't read anymore, the tears in my eyes distorting the letters with my insides suddenly coming to life. My mouth began to fill with saliva as my stomach cramped. I pushed myself off the couch and managed to run to the bathroom, where I dropped before the toilet bowl and, with one hand, flipped up the lid while bracing myself with the other. A hot, acidic stream of dread shot out of me, hitting the porcelain with enough force to spray some rogue drops back at me. The blackness of the coffee turned the water in the bowl into a putrid mess, and I squeezed my eyes shut in the hope of waking up in bed with a wet pillow beneath my head, which signified yet another nightmare.

The edge of the toilet was what I focused on, the coldness somehow signifying the reality of the situation. This wasn't a dream or a nightmare or anything else my brain could have conjured up. Brian Hurst was dead, and those glazed-over eyes staring back at me from the shadows had been confirmed. Seeing them once more turned my stomach again as a fresh wave of convulsions gripped me. I rose onto my knees and grabbed the toilet with my other hand, hanging on for my dear life as I let my body take over.

After my third round of vomiting, I finally managed to let go of the bowl and fall to the floor in a frightened heap as more tears streamed from me. I pulled my knees tightly in and closed my eyes, unable to shut out the ones continuing to taunt me from the recesses of my mind. Guilt began to flood over me; that donation page and those web images were just tormenting me.

I'm not sure how long I sat on the floor of my bathroom in complete shock before I eventually drifted off to sleep. Too many questions weaved in and out of my consciousness. The idea that I was somewhat responsible for the man's death was one of the most prevalent of all. But not all of my thoughts attacked me. Hiding in the background, barely bright enough to be seen, there hung one thought that didn't immediately make itself known. It was a question that would eventually take me in an entirely different direction.

Did I just get away with murder?

Chapter 6

Waking up seven hours after succumbing to the extreme fatigue on my bathroom floor came as no surprise to me. I knew just how devastating shock could be, having dealt with its after-effects multiple times during the course of my job. At first, I wasn't quite sure where I was, and the bathroom tiles felt deceptively cold. My first thought was that I might have gone to the mall and taken a fall, but the lack of crowd noise was what eventually made me snap open my eyes.

It took a bit of an effort to lift my head enough to look around. I could see the glow of the late afternoon sun through my open bathroom door, where it hung in the sky outside my living room balcony. There was no shopping mall, no one around, just the same vacant apartment with me on the floor. With my cell phone still on the floor in front of the couch, I wasn't sure what goals I had for that morning. However, I realized that any plans I had made for the day were unlikely to happen.

As I tried to process the lost time, that news story came back to memory; the photo of Neena Hurst sitting with her family, that one hit the hardest. My legs still felt shaky, and it took me a moment to convince myself that I could get up without falling over again. When I reached the couch, I first sat down and leaned over to pick up my phone. The screen lit up as one of my fingers ran across the surface, and I saw one missed call and two messages waiting for me.

Peg was the one who called, as indicated in one of the messages I received, while the other message only informed me about the missed call. Did you see that sleazy guy from the bar the other night died from a fall?? What the hell, and he had a family, was what she texted me. I closed my eyes and gripped the cell phone tight in my fingers as I pushed it into my forehead. It appeared as if there was no escape from this story. The phone suddenly vibrated in my fingers as another message came through, almost buzzing me back into reality.

Hey, where are you? Is everything OK?

It was another message from Peg, and I guiltily typed a response before she took the next step, which was to call me.

I had a day in bed. I'm not feeling the best.

She responded a few seconds later, just as I knew she would.

Do you want me to bring you anything? I don't start work for another couple of hours. To which I responded...

Nah, all good, thanks. I don't want to move.

I waited for another response for a couple of minutes, but once I was sure she wouldn't send one, I went to the kitchen and poured myself a glass of water. The coolness sent a shiver through me as it reached all the way down to my toes. I drank the entire glass in just a couple of gulps and ended up grabbing a second, and then I went back to the couch. Instead of trying to search for more information on my phone, I grabbed the laptop.

Once the screen powered up, I opened up a fresh Google page and began to type Hurst's name into the search bar but froze as a realization suddenly dawned on me. What if the sheriff was already watching me? Chills came over me as I remembered the reporter stating that a report would be released in the next couple of days. Why so long? Wouldn't a random accident be a simple open-and-shut case? Why would they need to wait...unless, of course, they had questions they still needed answering.

That was when the security cameras came back to mind, along with yet more questions I needed answers to, like why I hadn't been arrested yet. If those cameras did their job like they were supposed to, wouldn't they have captured the entire event?

Maybe they saw the way he attacked me and figured it was nothing more than a tragic accident brought on by the deceased himself.

"They'd still have questions, idiot," I told myself as I shook my head at the frustration of my brain again trying to throw out ill-conceived logic.

Staring down at the laptop screen, I wondered if my search history would be subpoenaed in court when they brought me to trial, a trial I had already envisioned multiple times. Or maybe it's just my internet history in general. Would they be able to bring up everything I'd looked at on my phone as well?

I suddenly remembered a couple of the internet security guys down at the hospital talking about how one of them was downloading illegal movies and how they needed something to hide their internet activity. Letters, that's what I recalled, one of them saying a bunch of letters that I couldn't remember. JKN? RPN?

"Definitely an N," I muttered to myself as I typed a new idea into the search bar.

How to hide your internet activity, was what I sent out into the void, and what came back were multiple articles and offers for what I now know to be a VPN service. I clicked on the first article and read a brief description of what the service provided. Once I was sure of what I needed, I clicked on one offering a 14-day Free Trial.

I went through the process of downloading the software package to my computer, then went through the installation process and through the necessary steps to ensure my privacy.

After I was sure I was good to go, I opened a new internet page and then turned on Incognito Mode just to add another layer to my already suspicious activities. I almost considered buying myself a new laptop but quickly decided that was just an expensive step into a possible over-reaction.

It took me a couple of hours, but what began as nothing more than an unplanned fishing trip for information quickly turned into a full-blown, choreographed investigation. I found one article, then found a second, and even a third. I navigated to The Silver Lining's webpage and found out who our bartender was that served us on the night of the…accident…on the website's Our Team page. I began searching social media for the guy. When I located him on Facebook, I quickly scrolled through his feed and found a post about him finding the body and how it made for a tough day on the job. One of the comments came from a family member telling him to stay strong.

Social media turned out to be my greatest ally as I found the comments sections of the posts to be where the real gold stands the tests of time. Random comments would be linked to certain services, and in a relatively small city, information wouldn't tend to remain hidden for long. I even found comments from consultants on a GoFundMe post, offering anybody affected some free counseling if they needed it.

By seven o'clock, my stomach began to growl, and I couldn't remember the last time I'd eaten something substantial. One look at my kitchen and I knew the last thing I wanted to do was cook, so after throwing on some jeans and shoes, I grabbed my phone and keys and headed out into the night.

Burger King ended up being my choice that night, and feeling like I had a rather large hole to fill, I ordered a double whopper with some onion rings. Fearing my blood sugar might drop to the kinds of levels that caused accidents, I pulled into a parking spot rather than head back home. In all honesty, judging from the way my fingers were shaking, I don't think I would have made it.

The burger was messy; between the mayonnaise and ketchup and everything sliding out, I should have asked for extra napkins. Either way, I finished the whopper in record time. I placed my bag of onion rings on the dash in front of me. I took my time; between the texture and the light crunch, they were delicious. After reaching for another, my eyes fell on the people sitting inside the restaurant.

People-watching wasn't exactly a pastime for me but I did often find it fascinating. There was just something captivating about watching people going about their lives doing the most mundane things imaginable, like standing in line at a fast-food restaurant. Old couples standing hand-in-hand, young boyfriends protectively holding their girlfriends close, moms watching their...

Sitting at a table near the back of the line was Neena Hurst, her two girls occupying the seats on either side of her. They each had a kid's meal in front of them; Ally was sipping her drink from a straw. What caught me by surprise wasn't seeing the family but rather seeing the...smiles on the girls' faces. From a distance, they looked just like the rest of the families seated around the restaurant with children, all happily united by some childhood experience.

Neena didn't precisely look overjoyed, but I did detect a kind of relief in her. She helped Grace with her drink before holding out a nugget for her, which she dipped in one of the sauces her mother held out. They looked like...a family again, one far from the broken mess that I had witnessed sitting in my examination room. The three of them blended in perfectly, acting no different than the rest of the people, maybe for the first time in a long time, reclaiming their place in society.

What I didn't know then and would only find out a couple of months later was that Neena Hurst took full advantage of her new-found freedom, a freedom she had never imagined possible for herself. The GoFundMe set up in their name ended up raising more than forty thousand dollars. After selling the junker as well as their family home, Neena used the money to move her family to a small town in central Missouri and made a fresh start. I still follow her social media posts from time to time but try not to get too engaged. A part of me wanted that image of the three of them sitting in that restaurant to be the one that I remembered most.

Chapter 7

The sheriff's office never ended up on my front door like I had imagined. Instead, I ended up reading a final report from the coroner that classed the death as accidental, caused by a combination of intoxication and an undiagnosed condition of Meniere's Disease. The latter carried with it sudden episodes of vertigo. It's believed that alcohol mixed with a loss of balance added to the situation that caused Brian Hurst to fall to his doom. No mention was ever made of a mystery woman struggling with him moments before his death. The cameras I had been so worried about turned out to be out-of-order, a condition they had endured for nearly a year due to the owner's lack of concern for repair costs and a greater focus on profits.

For me, I saw the camera situation as a blessing in disguise. While I couldn't exactly share the experience with anybody, I firmly believed that fate had chosen me personally. It found a way for me to free the family of the monster that had been terrorizing their lives for too long and give them a chance to start fresh.

The days of worrying about law enforcement coming to bring me in soon faded into memories, and I think I managed to get back to the same mundane life I had led before the Hurst incident. Work has a way of reminding you of your true role in the world, and as weeks turned into months, my existence became deeply intertwined with the walls of the emergency department.

By March of the following year, a few developments occurred, particularly with some colleagues I collaborated with advancing or transitioning within our organization. First, Fitzby ended up getting a promotion to running the Intensive Care Unit, a definite step up for him. He once told me that his ultimate goal was to one day sit in the director's chair and this was definitely a move in the right direction.

Alison ended up resigning from her position altogether and changed careers, so to speak. She ended up finding out that the crampiness she had been experiencing was in fact, an unplanned pregnancy. After working things out with Barry, she decided to relocate to Phoenix to be closer to her family.

Peg also ended up getting a promotion to shift supervisor, which was a definite step up for her. Funnily enough, when I put forth my name to change to permanent night shift, it was Peg who approved my request and essentially ended up becoming my new boss. We celebrated together, although I did suggest a bar at the other end of town. The Silver Lining just didn't feel like a place I could ever set foot in again. Something about stirring up memories was what drove me from the establishment. Who knew if the bartender might recognize me from that evening and then suddenly remember catching a glimpse of me walking out the back on the night of the unfortunate incident?

Anyway, I didn't want to tempt fate, despite it initially seeking me out. Instead, I decided that the best course of action was to simply get on with living my life. Maybe that was fate's plan all along because when the night of March 18 came around, I wondered whether it had other work for me to do.

"Liz, you've got a DV waiting for you in Six," is what Peg told me that early Sunday night.

The truth is, hearing those words chilled me to the bone, the reaction coming at me from multiple angles. The same nerves I had in the days following the Hurst accident returned in an instant, the fear of getting caught breaking out as beads of sweat across my brow.

"Liz?"

"Yes, I've got it," I said with a smile, forcing my feet into action after finding them refusing to respond to my commands. "Husband and wife in the room?"

"Just the wife. Husband's apparently out in the car."

Imagine the mental strength I needed to walk toward the door and then the physical strength just to open it. After taking one hell of a deep breath, I made my way into the room and was immediately struck by the similarities I had begun to recognize between the victims of domestic abuse.

Unlike many of the other domestic violence victims I'd treated in my time, Sophia Traiforos's husband not being in the room with her. It meant he had significant control over her. If he hadn't even bothered to come into the hospital with his wife, that meant he felt safe enough for her to deal with unwanted questions on her own.

It was apparent from the moment I saw her that the bottom lip needed at least a stitch. I couldn't see any other facial bruising, but that didn't mean much.

"Do you have pain anywhere else," I asked her as I prepared to clean her wound. She didn't answer immediately, instead narrowing her eyes to study me. "Do you understand English?"

"A little," she said with a thick accent.

The other thing I noticed about her almost immediately was the thick jumper she wore, not a common sight during mid-spring in Texas. Aged 59, I didn't think she suffered from the coldness older people endured from a lack of circulation.

She looked too young and in pretty decent shape, yet she still shielded herself with thermal layers.

Thinking outside the box, I decided to go a little unorthodox. I could have taken her blood pressure over the top of her sleeve, but I held up the arm strap to indicate my intention. She hesitated at first, and I didn't think she would play along, but after I paused with the strap dangling between us, I think she saw that I wasn't about to change my mind.

With a little bit of help from me, she pulled the jumper over the top of her head, and what I saw just about broke me. Not only did the bruises run along the length of her arms, but when her shirt rode a little up her back a little, it exposed yet more bruising. Not just fresh discoloration but bruise upon bruise from sustained beating.

"Please," the woman cried when she saw me staring at the injuries.

"Please, no say something."

"Mrs. Traiforos, I have to report this," I said, hoping by lowering my voice that I could push forth some empathy. Her eyes widened in horror.

"No, no, please." She grabbed my arm with trembling hands, her eyes filling with tears. "He no blame. Me, me."

"No, Mrs. Traiforos, please. What your husband is doing is illegal."

She began to cry uncontrollably, and I could see why her husband probably figured it was best to remain out in the car. The woman had barely the mental strength to shield her face with both hands, crying into them as she struggled to comprehend the enormity of the situation. I thought she would begin vomiting at any moment, her world suddenly crumbling the way I imagined Neena Hurst would have. And that was when I remembered the young mother sitting in a certain Burger King with her two daughters, a woman looking almost reborn.

"OK, I won't say anything," I finally managed, not because I felt sorry for her and definitely not because of her waiting husband.

No, the reason I agreed not to report the matter to the proper authorities was because I suddenly had an overwhelming sense of fate paying me another visit. I could feel it resting on my shoulder, watching as I dealt with yet another victim who probably had been suffering for many years without any help whatsoever. Neena Hurst's face appeared, both the pain during my initial examination and the relieved one enjoying a meal with her children.

I'm not sure at which point I came to the conclusion that I needed to help this woman, but what I do remember was the exact moment I saw myself *arranging* another accident. It happened when Sophia Traiforos removed the hands from her face and flashed the briefest hint of relief at me. The weight of the world suddenly lifted when she realized she wouldn't have to deal with the sheriff after all.

I think the stitch ended up being the least painful part of the visit for the lady, who would no doubt face an avalanche of questions the moment she climbed back into the car. When I finished treating her, I walked her back out to the waiting room. I considered escorting her to the car just to share a moment of eye contact with the monster responsible for her injuries. I didn't, of course. I knew that if I did, the woman would pay the price when she got home, and I wanted to save her from any unnecessary pain.

When I got back to the station, my first job was to update the patient's file with her latest treatment, and while my brain was still going at a million miles per minute, I put the opportunity to good use. Given the rules surrounding opening certain people's medical records, I knew this would be my one opportunity to get as much information as I could. If I didn't, then the chances of me gaining legitimate access again in the near future depended on Sophia Traiforos not only returning to the ED but also during one of my shifts.

None of the other nurses paid me the slightest attention as I began typing out the treatment. Peg wasn't around, and the only other nurse in the station was busy typing up her own report. From what I could see, it appeared that the woman had been to the hospital only once before, a visit two years earlier to treat a broken rib. Not exactly convincing evidence of abuse. The doctor who had treated her was Fitzby, and I understood why the matter hadn't gone further.

As I typed, I tried to take in as much as possible from other parts of the file, like the home address and any other family members. The name Benjamin Traiforos appeared in the spouse/partner window, and I waited until I finished updating the file before I clicked the link to his file. Accessing the file through a linked spouse's incident wasn't unusual. Medical staff did so all the time, especially when needing to find associated conditions or possible connections for emergency contact.

It took me all of two seconds to not only gain access to Sofia Traiforos's husband's records from his last year's visit, but also how I could potentially ease her suffering for good. Written in one of the first boxes of the file was the man's Level 1 Allergy to peanuts, a reaction he'd been admitted to hospital twice before. Each time, he'd been listed as critical, which meant exposure to any form had the potential to kill him.

When I shut down the file and logged myself out of the system again, the wheels of something new began to turn, slowly at first but definitely gaining momentum. I still wasn't entirely sure about what I was planning to do, but one thing was clear, the woman needed someone to step in and assist her. If I didn't, then Sophia would most likely end up becoming just another statistic whenever her husband finally lost control over whatever monster lived inside him.

I don't think I remember much of that night when the shift finally came to an end, and I headed out to my car. What stood out more than anything was the number of different scenarios. I'd already imagined how to help Sophia out of her situation.

The thought of me being seen as a murderer didn't even cross my mind, or at least not at that stage. All I could see were the unfortunate victims who'd been dedicated to these bad relationships and ended up as nothing more than punching bags. These were the people who needed my help; their own lives were nothing more than a living hell from which there seemed no escape. How could I turn my back on them when it appeared as if I had been given a purpose, sent by fate itself to intervene and help them finally flee?

The sun was just beginning to rise over the distant horizon when I pulled into my building's parking lot. I paused long enough to appreciate the brilliant explosion of color as the sun's rays hit a couple of solitary clouds and reflected a kaleidoscope of fire across the sky. What I saw in that sunrise was a new beginning, not for me but for a woman who remained trapped in her own personal nightmare, one that I hoped I could help her escape from.

Chapter 8

While I knew I had a job to do, I still needed to ensure my own life continued on as if nothing had changed. If people began noticing a distinct change in me, then they might start to ask questions, and I didn't think my alibis would hold up for very long under scrutiny.

The urge to sit right down the second I walked through my door and began planning another monster's demise was almost impossible to ignore. Still, I resisted the temptation by trying to stick to my usual routine after a night shift. Unlike a day shift, where I would go home, have dinner, and then chill on the couch until bedtime, my routine after a night shift paled in comparison. Depending on my level of fatigue, the first thing I did was collapse onto the bed, close my eyes, and sleep until I got some serious rest.

This particular morning proved almost the same, the only difference being a quick shower. Some mornings, I just felt like I needed to wash the shift off my skin, especially when working through a cocktail of unpleasant patients. There was only so much bullshit a nurse could take from drunks and junkies before needing a de-cleanse.

The shower did exactly what I needed it to, as far as washing off the unpleasant shift, but it did little to distract me from what remained at the forefront of my mind. Benjamin Traiforos was a name now dominating my thoughts, and I knew that the urge to deal with him would only get worse the longer I put things off.

The one thing I stopped using since changing to the night shift was my alarm. For one, I didn't seem to need it. My body clock just seemed to kick in at just the right time each afternoon, and I found myself usually waking up ten to fifteen minutes before whatever time I had set it for. The other thing I discovered was that I felt a lot more refreshed waking up naturally instead of to the sounds of some high-screeching annoyance.

I noticed since swapping to nights was how much easier sleep seemed for me. No more tossing and turning or waiting for my body to finally let go of the day's frustrations. Some mornings, I'd barely remember lying in bed at all, my eyes closing the instant my head hit the pillow, and boom, lights out. No trying to get comfortable, no staring into the darkness and hoping to drift off before time ran out. I just felt like a unified force of cohesion.

When I woke up later that afternoon to the sound of some truck honking its horn out on the interstate, the first thing I thought the instant my eyes opened was how I needed to get to know this Ben fellow. While not exactly positive, I had the faintest memory of dreaming about tracking him and finding out that he lived a fake life with another wife in a nearby town. Of course I wasn't expecting to find any truth to the dream, but I have to admit that when I opened my laptop while still lying in bed, I did wonder whether such a thing was possible.

I must have spent almost an hour searching for anything I could find on the Traiforos family, but it appeared that none of them had any sort of social media profile, which was a surprise given our day and age. I did find a John Traiforos over in Midland, Texas, but I couldn't see anything suggesting he was related to the one I was after.

Feeling more than a little frustrated with myself, I jumped out of bed and fixed myself a cup of coffee. While the machine went to work, I opted for a bit of food as well, the grumbling in my stomach a sign of the lack of food I'd had since the previous afternoon. Twenty minutes later, I sat down with a plate of scrambled eggs and bacon, the coffee, and the laptop for company. I couldn't exactly afford to waste a lot of time, so I figured multi-tasking was perhaps my best option.

I continued searching the internet while eating my breakfast, looking for any sign of Benjamin Traiforos. It was only when I decided to check the street view of the address I memorized from the files that I finally managed to get some sort of breakthrough. Parked in the driveway of the modest home sat an old pickup truck, some cheap magnetic signage on the doors advertising a plumbing business.

Ben the Friendly Plumber, was the name on the signs, and after a quick search, I found that the business wasn't registered with any of the usual departments. There was also something about the name itself that irritated the hell out of me. I imagined a warm and fuzzy guy rolling up in his pickup truck, ready to quote for a job. He'd possess all the usual charm, warm smile, and tight handshake. He'd laugh and make jokes, give his clients the sense that he was just a down-to-earth lovable guy when in fact, he loved nothing more than to go home and beat the shit out of his wife.

When I checked the time and saw that it was already after five, I knew that Ben would have to wait for another day. After shutting down the internet page and wiping the history, I closed the laptop, took my empty cup and plate to the sink, and washed them clean. Leaving the dishes to dry on the rack, I headed back to the bedroom and began to get myself ready for another shift.

The regular night shift wasn't like the usual standard cycle roster. Our night shift staff worked the full twelve-hour rotation instead of the expected eight of regular occupations. We also had four fewer staff members on our roster, which made for a much more interesting shift. More work, fewer workers was how Peg described it to me when she suggested I make the switch, wanting to make sure I knew what I was signing up for ahead of time.

I didn't mind. Hard work never hurt anybody, and I actually preferred the night shift over days. For one, nights meant far fewer managers around. With most of the administration on another shift, it signified only those working the actual floor remained. It also represented how we found ourselves a lot busier than usual, which made the time absolutely fly by. Much better than sitting around twiddling one's thumbs.

And if all that wasn't enough, I also found that I really loved the people I worked with. Peg was a given, of course, one of my closest friends. Mackenzie was another one who made the switch when she heard I was transitioning over. Throw in Andy Lambert, Jas Chang, Lila Tumber, Vanessa Zhou, and the adopted mother to us all, Ruth Lin, and we had a really good team.

The doctors weren't too bad either, although just being away from Fitzby more than made up for whoever else we got stuck with. The doctors also tended to cycle through the ED a lot more, so we weren't always sure of who would show up. We each had our favorites, of course, with me absolutely loving a little firecracker doctor named Lila Raja. Originally from Mumbai, Lila moved to Odessa a year earlier. She already made quite a name for herself by being one of the few who knew exactly how to speak to junkies trying to score medications through the ED.

Working from six until six also had significant downsides. It wasn't all high-fives and backslaps. Most nights, the ambulances had to get in line in order to be unloaded, but not unless they carried a critical patient. The waiting room wasn't much better, with a lot of the people spending hours upon hours waiting to see a doctor. Again, the people ranked and organized according to the severity of their issues.

This particular night turned out to be one of the better ones, and it felt like an absolute cruise compared to many other nights. Lila told me it had something to do with the moon's cycle, and Andy backed her up, claiming that it was a verifiable fact that nights without any moon at all always proved less stressful than full moons. I wasn't sure; I was not one to pay attention to that kind of stuff. But we already know of other staff members who also felt the same way.

The worst part of the night came when an elderly gentleman suffering from chest pain came in via ambulance. He lived out on a ranch some twenty miles out of town with his wife, and for some reason, she decided to drive herself to the hospital so the truck would be there for them when he got released the following morning. Despite our best efforts,

Gerry Hartwell passed away five minutes before his wife of sixty years made it there. It was Lila who greeted her in the waiting room and immediately walked her into a more private room to deliver the news.

I'm not sure whether it's common knowledge, but every hospital has a chapel located somewhere within its walls. That was where I found Bethany Hartwell sitting quietly alone when I headed to the lunchroom shortly after four in the morning. I considered not disturbing the grieving widow, but she spotted me standing near the door, and when we exchanged a smile, I knew I couldn't just walk away.

"I'm so sorry for your loss," I said as I slid in beside her after Bethany patted the seat next to her.

"Thank you, love, but Gerry and I had prepared for this night long ago," she said as she looked up at the cross hanging on the wall.

"He's had heart issues for the last ten years."

"Still, I guess it's not easy."

"Oh, death never is," she said with a smile. "But when you've faced it as often as we have, I guess it just becomes a part of life." When she saw that I wasn't following, she elaborated. "When you get to our age, death is no longer a stranger. It might not feel right, but it's the one guarantee we all have, the one part of life we're all promised to meet when our time comes. Gerry wished me goodbye just like he had the last couple of times we'd come to the hospital." She grinned and shook her head. "It was his idea for me to drive so that I had a vehicle to get back home in case he fell off the perch this time." Now, it was my time to chuckle.

"I guess he really did fall off the perch this time."

"That he did."

"He told me you had been married for sixty years. That's certainly a decent stretch," I said.

"Not nearly as long as you might imagine," Beth said with another smile. "Time flies when you're lucky enough to be living your best life."

"Is that what you had?"

"Oh, yes, for sure." She paused for a few seconds. "I couldn't imagine how things would have turned out if I'd stayed with my first husband."

"Gerry wasn't your first?" The revelation caught me by surprise.

"Oh no, we married about a year after my first husband died in a car accident."

"Oh, I'm...so sorry."

"Don't be. Julius was an asshole." I almost broke into laughter hearing her curse but managed to hold it in. "He used to treat me like a piece of farming equipment. Got physical with me a few times too."

"Your ex-husband beat you?"

"Here and there, yes. It wasn't as talked about back then as it is today. My father certainly wouldn't have held back if he had known what was going on."

"How did Julius die?"

"Lost control on a bend and went over a cliff. Police believe his brakes might have failed, but they couldn't be sure. Fire destroyed most of the car."

Goosebumps broke out across my arms as I heard her describe a situation I thought I immediately recognized. While I couldn't be sure, I did picture the unknown face of her father watching his daughter's abuser drive right off that cliff in a car he'd fixed to fail. I imagined him cheering as the wreck burned on its way down to some unseen ravine where it would have smoldered until authorities managed to get to it if they ever did.

"Well, I guess it worked for you in the end then," I said. "Marrying a man like Gerry, I mean."

"I guess it did," she replied as I spotted a single tear roll down her far cheek. "But time eventually caught up, I guess."

"That it did," I said. "But at least you still carry the positive memories."

"Those I'll cherish forever," Beth said, and that was when I saw her bottom lip tremble enough to indicate that she needed some alone time. I gave her shoulder a light squeeze, thanked her for chatting with me, and continued on my way.

It may not sound like it to you, but to me, hearing Bethany Hartwell describe her first and only abuser meet an untimely death felt like fate again, tapping me on the shoulder. A mild push to let me know I was moving in the right direction. When I walked past the chapel shortly after grabbing a quick bite, the grieving widow was gone, no doubt making her way back to the empty home waiting for her.

I continued through the rest of my shift, but it somehow felt like I was working on autopilot as my brain detached itself from my surroundings. With Beth Hartwell in my heart and Ben Traiforos in my head, I found myself constantly thinking about all the possible ways for me to end him and ensure that whatever life Sophia still had would be lived in relative comfort.

When I walked out of the hospital just after six that morning, a thick band of cloud stretched across the sky, blocking any chance for a colorful sunrise. I reached my car with a few spots of rain falling and by the time I turned onto the road, a decent shower began to fall on the city. Refusing to let the weather deter me, I didn't slow as I raced to get home and prepare for the day ahead.

The one decision I made during those final hours of my shift was not to bother with sleep. Not on the day I intended to get a better handle on Ben. Once home, I barely slowed down as I raced into the bathroom and jumped in the shower.

After a very quick scrub, I wrapped the towel around me and headed to the bedroom, where I grabbed some jeans and a t-shirt.

From what I could tell, Ben worked for himself, and that indicated he decided his own schedule. Contractors like him usually didn't have a set start and finish time, which meant I had a bit more work to do. My plan was to start with a simple drive-by of their house to see whether he was home or not. If he was, I planned to find a spot to park that was close enough for me to maintain a visual of the home. If the vehicle wasn't present, then I planned to return earlier the following morning and see if I could catch him.

Again, pushing my car to the very edge of the speed limit, I raced to the other side of the city to where I had memorized their home to be, the house sitting on Idlewood Street. Thankfully, traffic hadn't yet picked up, and I managed to get to the neighborhood well before seven that morning. As it turned out, the wife-beater hadn't left for work.

With the home's driveway facing the street, I first drove past the house and continued for three blocks before turning the car around. Two blocks away from the house, I pulled next to the curb and made myself comfortable, ensuring I maintained a clear line of sight with the residence.

It quickly became apparent to me that I hadn't thought the situation through enough. To be honest, it was my very first stakeout, so I hadn't exactly considered the possible hours I'd be stuck in the car. With no food or drink to speak of, how long would I be able to sit in the open sun once the day's heat began to pick up? And then there was the whole bathroom situation to work through.

"I don't care," I said out loud as I watched a cab drive past. "I am not moving until I absolutely have to."

One thing you might not have realized about me is that I tend to be incredibly persistent when I focus on something. If I knew I had to work my way through something, you could rest assured that I wouldn't stop until my goal had been achieved, and staking out abusive husbands was a new addition to my list. Thankfully, it turned out that I didn't have to wait quite as long as I imagined. Just twenty minutes after showing up, I watched a large man emerge from the house and walk to the truck. He tossed something into the tray of the pickup before climbing into the cab.

Ben looked enormous even from my distant vantage point. He stood a good six inches above the roof of his truck, which must have put his overall height somewhere north of six-foot-five. He also weighed a considerable sum and I saw the truck definitely tilt slightly when he stepped into the cabin. A thick cloud of exhaust smoke blew out of the exhaustive pipe, and when he reversed onto the street, I started my engine.

Following the truck wasn't an issue for the first few miles, not with the lack of traffic and us managing to hit every green light along the way. The first real challenge came when we reached the very top of Parkway Boulevard, and Ben pulled into a lonely gas station sitting a quarter mile from the entrance ramp to the 338. Because of the lack of other cars on the road, I considered continuing on but didn't want to risk losing sight of him so I pulled in beside one of the pumps and headed inside.

While I went to the row of fridges, Ben first waved to the cashier behind the counter, then headed to the coffee machine and made himself a cappuccino. I grabbed myself a can of Coke before heading to the candy bar aisle to pretend to search for something to munch on. Once he had his coffee ready, Ben walked to the baked goods display, grabbed himself a chocolate iced donut, and popped it into a paper bag before taking his goods up to the counter.

During the brief moment I stood in the candy bar aisle, I took a quick look around for any security cameras. There was one directly behind the counter aiming down at whoever stood to be served, but I couldn't see any others covering the rest of the store. It felt like the first positive break for me.

When another customer walked through the door, I grabbed a random candy bar and hurried to stand behind Ben. The last thing I wanted was to get stuck behind someone else. If there was one thing I knew about the smaller type of gas stations, it was that the cashiers always knew their regular customers.

"Just my usual, Norm," I heard Ben tell the cashier before handing over a twenty. He looked around and met the eyes of the customer behind me and gave him a head nod before turning back to receive his change. I stood my ground and pretended to be staring at my phone to avoid having to look at him.

Ben thanked Norm again as he grabbed his change and casually walked out. I dropped the drink and candy bar onto the counter and held my cash out, hoping to make a quick transaction, but that was when the cashier had other ideas.

"I'm sorry, one sec," he said, and before I had a chance to say anything, he suddenly walked out from behind the counter and went to the far back corner of the store, where he disappeared into a back office.

Faced with an impossible choice, I watched as Ben climbed back into his truck, started the engine a few moments later, and slowly rolled out of the gas station. I could have dropped the goods on the counter and ran back to my car, but stakeouts meant I was not pulling unwanted attention, right?

"Sorry about that," the cashier said just as I watched the truck disappear from view, his return narrowing down my options.

With panic setting in, I held out the twenty and watched the man process the transaction, doing my best to keep the frustration hidden from view. I almost grabbed the goods and ran, ready to tell him to keep the change, but again, I reminded myself of the need to remain inconspicuous.

"Thank you, Ma'am," the cashier told me, and after a brief smile, he turned his attention to the next person in line.

I think I waited until the final few steps before I raced to the door of my car, ripped it open, and in one move, slipped behind the wheel and stuck the key into the ignition. I grabbed the seatbelt and shifted into gear at the same time, and hauled my butt out of the station. The problem was trying to figure out which way Ben went.

The 338 interchange proved to offer just two choices, north or south, and I didn't have a lot of time to decide which to take. I ended up opting for the left turn, as we had already traveled in that general direction for the previous few miles. I figured backtracking didn't make sense when heading north seemed to continue our original path.

As I accelerated hard up the on-ramp to try and make up some distance, I began to run the interaction back through my mind in the hope of storing every minute detail. The one thing I had picked up through countless hours of true crime television was that details mattered when it came to investigations, and that's exactly what I saw this as.

The one thing that immediately stood out to me was what Ben told the cashier when he first walked up to the counter.

Just my usual, Norm, was what he told him, which meant it wasn't just some random stop. While the times might have varied, it sounded as if the gas station was a place where the plumber stopped quite regularly.

I was still trying to think of anything else I might have picked up during the brief exchange when I spotted the rusted yellow tailgate of the Ford in the distance. From the looks of it, Ben wasn't much of a speed demon when it came to driving. Slowing down to match his speed, I put him down as someone who cruised along maybe five miles under the limit, just enough to frustrate those around him.

Making sure to keep plenty of distance between us, I kept a truck and a couple of cars in front of me, although they quickly caught up with the Ford and passed him by. I was trying to fall back enough for an approaching van to catch up to us, but that was when Ben took the next exit ramp. I slowed as much as I could to maintain at least a quarter-mile gap, but as it turned out, I didn't need to.

The place where the plumber appeared to be working was a new housing estate, the construction site encompassing almost a dozen blocks, each made up of varying degrees of newly constructed homes. The Ford made its way down the very middle of the zone before pulling over in front of half a dozen completed townhouses. I didn't need to enter the construction area at all, and I was able to see the truck from almost four blocks away.

With no reason to hang around, I ended up leaving just a couple of minutes after seeing the area, figuring that I'd found one of the answers I came looking for. What I now needed was to try and find a way of ending that monster's life without anybody suspecting foul play, an easier thing to think of than actually plan out.

I used the time it took to drive home as my starting point, thinking about all the possible ways I could kill him. The first problem I had almost immediately was thinking about those exact words. What was I really planning to do? To kill him? It sounded impossibly evil to me. Not only that, but it also sounded wrong. Brian Hurst had been nothing more than an accidental death. How had I suddenly evolved from that accident to now planning an actual murder?

"Because Sophia needs you to save her," was what I whispered under my breath to remind myself of the objective. To try and back up my words, I brought forth the memory of Sophia's bruise-covered arms, the hideous purple-yellow smears running along her back where her husband had landed either punches, kicks, or a combination of both, who knows.

Regardless of how brutish or evil it sounded, this wasn't some sick serial killer looking to get their kicks. This wasn't an urge to satisfy a hunger for blood or whatever else that drives murderers. This was me trying to free a woman from years of abuse who deserved at least a few years of peace. This was fate enabling me to help rid the world of a monster.

.

Chapter 9

Trying to find a way of killing someone without drawing attention to the act turned out to be an almost impossible task to figure out. Remembering my conversation with Bethany Hartwell, I quickly realized that unlike the moment in time when I suspected her father took care of a certain asshole, modern technology proved to be my undoing. Tampering with someone's brakes wasn't as simple as it was back then, and even if I could, how do I make it appear accidental?

Not only that, but I had modern technology to deal with, like cameras, and cell phone tracking, vehicle tracking, as well as the science crime fighters used to bust criminals. Even if I did manage to kill the man, the slightest suspicion would unleash an absolute arsenal of crime-fighting techniques.

No, I had to find a way to end him completely by accident, a way that investigators wouldn't even think of questioning. By the time I returned to my apartment after my early morning drive, the only decision I had reached was that whatever I chose to do would need to involve something that typically claimed lives. Brake failure wasn't something I believed to be a viable option.

Fatigue hit me pretty hard after I dropped onto the couch, and within a few minutes, I pushed a couple of cushions into the armrest and laid down. The plan was to just rest my head for a little bit, but who was I kidding? The next thing I knew, my cell phone was ringing somewhere next to my head, and when I blindly answered it while struggling to open my eyes, the caller simply hung up.

Imagine my surprise when I saw that I'd been asleep for almost nine hours, the sun already well on the way to calling it quits on another day. Thankfully, I wasn't scheduled for work, so I had the night free to continue trying to work out the best way of enabling my plan. I barely got my eyes open when I suddenly had an epiphany; a moment of two thoughts suddenly collided violently enough for me to sit upright in deep contemplation.

"The donut," were the words I muttered, verbalizing the image in my head.

The brief minuscule moment of clarity carried two thoughts within it, the scene where Ben reached the counter and told the cashier he had his usual order and the scene of me opening up the man's medical record to find he was allergic to peanuts. All I could do was stare into the space between the wall and me as a myriad of possibilities suddenly came to life in my head. If I could find a way to bring the two visions together then I was almost sure I could arrange an accident nobody would assume to be orchestrated.

Despite the veil of sleepy brain fog still hanging over me, I reached over and snatched up my laptop from the coffee table. After leaning back into the couch, I set the computer on my lap and whipped the lid open. The screen came to life, and by the time I'd given both eyes a good rub with the backs of my hands, my little workhorse was good to go.

Once I'd set up the VPN and opened an incognito window, I began researching peanut allergies. The issue I faced was that I didn't believe it would be possible to add anything to the man's coffee. But a donut might be a different story. The issue I had was that chocolate donuts didn't tend to have peanuts in them. I needed to find a way of bringing the two components together in a way that would, firstly, not get noticed by Ben and secondly, not be seen as intentional by the medical examiner who would ultimately perform an autopsy on the man.

Instead of looking deeper into the peanut allergy per se, I switched directions and began looking into the company that made the chocolate donut, a local bakery named Holey Delights. The company supplied most of the gas stations and truck stops within the greater Ector County area with an array of baked goods, most notably a dozen different varieties of donuts. Running my eyes down the list of flavors, I found the one I was hoping for, the only flavor I was about to become an expert on. The photo of the donut was enough to get my mouth watering, but the description truly made me want one.

Enjoy our delectable Peanut Fudge Donuts featuring a rich and decadent peanut butter and chocolate fondant center, finished with a delicious loop of smooth chocolate-peanut sweet frost and peanut sprinkles.

Yup, it definitely wasn't the choice of flavor Ben would ever go for, but just reading the description was enough to awaken my own stomach, the growls rising in the silence of my apartment. Running my eyes over the list of ingredients, they stopped on one in particular, perhaps the only one that would make my plan possible...peanut oil.

Feeling a hint of excitement at the possibility of my plan finally coming together, I ran a search on peanut oil but quickly found my short-lived excitement fading a moment later when I learned that peanut oil didn't cause allergic reactions due to its method of refinement. As it turned out, it was specific types of proteins that caused the reactions, and peanut oil didn't contain them.

"Damn it," I muttered under my breath as I set the laptop down on the coffee table and headed for the bathroom. "Back to the drawing board."

What I needed was some caffeine in my system, and after I finished emptying my bladder, I headed to the kitchen with plans to fill it again with the good stuff. Coffee always helped with my mental clarity, and I added a little extra scoop for a bit more kick. Several minutes later, I was back on the couch, laptop on my lap, coffee in one hand and scrolling with the other.

It took me another couple of hours of invested research, but what I discovered was that the bakery prided itself on using purely organic ingredients wherever possible. Holey Delights also donated extensively to local charities, the owner coming from a poverty-stricken background himself. I felt almost bad for needing to use the company for my plan, but I knew I had more important goals to meet.

What I eventually found was that peanut flour or meal would be my best chance of getting some of the potentially lethal protein into Traiforos's system. I figured that if I could mix enough of it into a small batch of sweet frost and then somehow spread it onto the donuts, then that might be a way for me to trick the man into unknowingly eating one. The question was how?

I ended up closing the laptop and sitting there with it in my lap as I thought about the gas station. With no cameras covering the part of the store where the baked goods were displayed, I'd have easy enough access to the donuts. I struggled to assess the timing, especially in determining whether the abuser would actually arrive on any given morning. We pulled into the gas station at precisely 7:34, and he reached his worksite at 7:48. That meant he had a starting time of 8:00, if my guess was correct.

Checking through online shopping portals, I uncovered that I preferred using peanut powder as opposed to peanut flour, as one retained nearly all of the original peanut kernel. I hoped it would add a bit more of a kick for when the monster swallowed a nice mouthful and ultimately choked on it. I was already picturing him sitting down with others for lunch and then falling off his chair after taking a bite.

Feeling a kind of urgency to get things moving, I ended up getting dressed and headed over to Gardendale. My guilty conscience kept me from going to something local. Or maybe it was the thought of law enforcement following any possible leads, like someone buying peanut powder the day before a resident died from an allergic reaction.

I ended up not only buying a half-pound bag of peanut powder but also everything else I needed for the sweet frost. Along the way, I stopped in at another gas station and bought a number of donut varieties, one being the chocolate frost variety and the other the fabled Peanut Fudge. I also picked up half a dozen plain ones that would support my final creation.

When I got back to my apartment, I immediately went to work, first tasting each donut, and then preparing a frosting I hoped would match the manufacturer's. The one thing I quickly found out was that there was a reason food makers hung tightly onto their recipes. Boy, was it difficult trying to get it to taste the same. I once read that Coca-Cola kept its recipe locked inside an actual bank vault they had built inside its building. Holey Delights didn't exactly compare to the likes of Coca-Cola, but it was still no easy task to mimic their recipe.

It took me until almost two in the morning before I had anything remotely close, and even then, I still had the issue of tasting peanuts in the frosting. I'd read that it didn't take much at all for a person to suffer a reaction, but then again, every person was different. Another couple of hours later, I think I had the right amount to work with, a delicate balance between the allergen and the sweet treat.

When I took my latest coffee out onto the balcony to watch the sunrise, I felt absolutely exhausted, almost as if I'd just finished a full-on shift in the ED. While it might not have been as physical, it certainly had been mentally exhausting, my brain feeling a little like jello. It felt nice to get a moment to sit, although my brain didn't stop. I still had the rest of the plan to work through.

What I envisioned was me hiding the half a dozen fake donuts in my jacket and then placing them inside the display cabinet right as Ben pulled up in his truck. It was too early, and I risked someone else buying one, perhaps an innocent mom or even a child ending up eating something they weren't expecting. The last thing I wanted to do was end up hurting some poor, innocent soul.

I headed back inside just after six and headed to the bedroom to get changed. Once happy with how I looked carrying my lethal cargo, I grabbed the rest of my things and headed out into the morning. My biggest issue, as I saw it, was not knowing whether Ben went to work every day. I figured I could spend another few days watching him, of course, but that meant subjecting his wife to yet more abuse, abuse I had the power to put an end to.

"It'll work out," I told myself as I jumped into my Civic, figuring that the worst course of action was to do nothing. I decided that if Ben didn't turn up, then the worst thing that would happen would be me buying my own donuts and taking them out again. I'd come home, go out that night for some fresh ones, and repeat the process every day until I succeeded. If there was one thing I was sure of, it was that Benjamin Traiforos's days were numbered.

I ended up pulling into a side street a couple of blocks from the gas station. It turned out that my timing had been way out, and I still had at least twenty minutes before I expected Ben to turn up...if he turned up at all. If my timing was off or he got delayed, I'd be forced to wait inside the store for too long before the cashier would grow suspicious. The one thing I needed to avoid at all costs was suspicions.

Time seemed to stall completely as I sat on that random suburban street, with each passing minute feeling more like an hour. I also felt a dull cramping down in the very pit of my stomach, a sensation I recognized as nerves. To try and distract myself, I turned on the radio, but after scanning through a couple of channels, I found the music more annoying than anything, so I switched it off again.

At precisely 7:27, I made my move, putting the car back into gear and rolling to the end of the street. It felt a little like some black ops mission I'd seen on TV, the only thing missing being the dramatic background melody. The beating in my chest was already well above average when I turned back onto the main street and kicked up considerably when the gas station came into view.

Two other cars sat parked at the fuel pumps and to try and make myself look a little more legit than the last time I was there, I decided to pump a few dollars worth of gas into my car. I figured if I appeared to have a purpose, then maybe anybody watching would look past me. I think it was the

Pay-At-The-Pump feature that gave me the idea, although I knew time wasn't my friend.

Seven bucks was all I managed to fit in my tank before my car halted to take any more. I'd only filled the tank a couple of days earlier, and given my lack of mileage, I hadn't really used it a lot. Once I returned the nozzle and closed my fuel flap, I headed inside, carefully concealing the rogue baked goods in the pit of my arm.

Once inside, I found Norm, the cashier, in deep conversation with one of the car owners, the other customer busy making himself a coffee. With the baked goods display right next to the beverage station, it made my next move near impossible. I looked nervously behind me to see whether the familiar Ford pickup had already arrived, but it wasn't anywhere to be seen, a small mercy given the situation.

Faced with a need to wait, I once again headed back to the candy bar section to pretend to be going through the variety of options. At the same time, the coffee customer continued to create whatever concoction his tastebuds desired. I was beginning to think that panic and frustration went hand in hand with trying to do fate's work, but that was when things took another turn.

Two things happened at exactly the same time. Taking another casual look out through the store window, I saw the familiar yellow-rusted Ford roll into the same parking space as the previous morning. Thinking I'd run out of time, I turned to face the back and saw the coffee guy finally finished making his drink. He started walking away to the counter, where Norm and his customer continued checking. Glancing out the window, I saw Ben in motion, leaving the yellow truck and walking to the doors. Nobody paid me the slightest attention.

My heart raced as I moved quickly to the end of the aisle. I slid my hand inside my jacket and pulled out the plastic container, which I fitted with a lid that kept the contents from spilling out while giving me silent access. With three spiked donuts in the container, I moved all of them in front of the three already inside the display, being careful to avoid touching the sweet frost. To make sure he went for his coffee first, I stood in front of the donut display, picked up some tongs and a small paper bag, and began to ponder over the choices like a regular customer. After greeting the cashier, Ben passed behind me, and it felt like all of the pieces had finally fallen into place. All that was left was for me to make my move and bring the whole game together.

I saw Ben drop something into the trashcan beside him out of the corner of my eye and figured it to be the stirrer, which meant he was finished. I figured having three tempting chocolate donuts in there was better than nothing. To give my standing there some credibility, I reached for a jelly-filled donut and slid it into the bag before stepping back.

"Those are the best," a voice suddenly said from beside me, and I looked up at the face of the man I planned to kill.

"I'm more of a chocolate fan," I said," but this is for my grandma."

"Well, tell her she's missing out," he said as he reached for the tongs, grabbed one of my recent additions, and popped it into his bag.

"I will,' I said, giving him a forced smile, and picked up another bag as Ben headed to the counter where Norm invited him into the conversation.

By the time I grabbed the two remaining spiked donuts and slid them into a separate bag, Norm had finished serving Ben and resumed his conversation. I returned the tongs and made my way to the cash register, where Norm tallied up my goods. I didn't want to make my urgency obvious, but when I reached the door and walked outside, I picked up the pace quite a bit.

I couldn't help but yank out that jelly donut while leaving the gas station. Already knowing this donut was going to be delicious, I took a big bite, realizing how much powdered sugar was on my fingers. Remembering how slowly Ben drives. I didn't exactly race to catch up with him, but I followed my heading at the speed limit once I got on the expressway.

While not exactly nervous, I did find my heart rate refusing to slow. I think it was the anticipation of what might happen.

In my mind, I'd imagined sitting way back from the building site and camping out until Ben ate that donut with his morning coffee. If my peanut-chocolate formula turned out to be the right mixture, I expected an ambulance to arrive at his workplace. They would likely search around to determine which of the new developments he was in, costing more time. What I wasn't expecting was to suddenly see his truck pulled over and parked in the breakdown lane with his right blinker flashing repetitively.

A sudden rush of panic hit me as I neared the truck, slowed down enough to get a good look inside the interior of the cabin, and then found what appeared to be an empty driver's seat. The window had been wound down, so I did get a good look inside but didn't see a sign of the driver. A few other cars passed me by as I tried to look over my shoulder, thinking that perhaps he'd pulled over for an unintended bathroom break. There were a couple of trees nearby but no sign of anybody using them for modesty's sake.

The panic didn't abate when the truck disappeared from my rearview mirror, turning into full-blown fear as I continued on my way down the road. I considered turning around but then knew it would only highlight me to anybody later checking through the footage. Instead, I continued on until

I reached the interchange with 385, took the exit, and then immediately rejoined the traffic heading south on 338.

I could feel my fingers gripping the wheel tight enough, wondering if I was going to leave an impression on the rubber. The one question that kept rolling over and over in my mind was whether I had just killed another man. When I finally came over a rise and saw the Ford in the distance again, more questions arose, questions I didn't even anticipate. Not only was there a huge truck parked in the adjoining lane next to Ben's vehicle about twenty yards further up, but there were also other cars pulled over, effectively shutting down all northbound traffic.

Again, I found myself slowing down so I could see what was happening over there. A couple of cars on my side of the parkway had also pulled over, their occupants crossing the median strip to join the small crowd surrounding something near the back wheels of the trailer. Here I was on the other side of traffic, staring at the scene; I saw that the driver's side door of the Ford hung open, the cabin empty. Tangled between the two rear sets of tires was something looking more like a crumpled heap, the pile displaying the same shirt Ben had been wearing just minutes earlier while buying his morning coffee.

There was blood...a lot of blood. One of the viewers stood away from the rest and appeared to be vomiting, while another was down on his knees, staring at the road and shaking his head. Others looked deathly grieving; the shock of Ben's mutilated body turned many spectators into a shaking mess. If there was one thing that I knew during those brief seconds of looking at the scene from my passing car it was that Benjamin Traiforos was no more. The days of him tormenting his unfortunate wife had come to an end. The question that remained in my mind was how.

Chapter 10

It took almost an hour for the first traffic report to come through, indicating that northbound traffic on Loop 338 had been closed due to a fatality. I know because I kept my ears glued to the radio the entire trip home and then turned both the radio and television on the second I stepped into my apartment. My heart skipped a beat when the radio DJ explained the traffic chaos to the listeners, but it just about stopped when I saw a News Alert flash on the television screen.

I'm fairly certain I held my breath the entire duration of listening to the news anchor share the details of a tragic fatality on the highway. According to eyewitnesses, a man in his late fifties appeared to jump out of his truck for unknown reasons just as a semi-trailer passed by, and tragically, he ended up getting sucked into the tires, where he died instantly.

The bulletin crossed for a live shot of the scene, and an on-site reporter interviewed the man I had seen vomiting earlier, although he appeared a lot fresher. He described the accident as happening almost instantly, having been behind the truck at the time of the collision. When the interview ended, and the reporter continued her report, she shared that initial indications pointed to the unfortunate victim. The man was possibly suffering from a medical episode, causing him to leave the vehicle. However, it was too early to tell.

I couldn't believe it. Ben Traiforos really was dead. While I couldn't be sure of his widow's reaction, my own verged on contentment. Not quite jubilation the way I had imagined, but I was definitely content knowing he would no longer hurt his wife. Had I really helped two helpless women escape abusive relationships by orchestrating the deaths of their abusers?

OK, I know the first wasn't exactly planned, but in a way, me walking out onto that loading dock did kind of seal Hurst's fate. Yes, he instigated the attack by trying to grab me, but it would never have happened if I hadn't gone out to confront him in the first place.

You might see it differently, but from where I was sitting, I'd set the wheels in motion for both men to die. Did they deserve it? I guess that's another debate best left for those with an opinion on how bad domestic abuse really is. To me, they deserved every bit and then some.

What I felt sitting there watching that report can only be described as stunned disbelief. When I sat through the rest of the news bulletin, staring into the space between the screen and me, all I could picture was me being tried as a serial killer. Did two victims make me one? If not, how many would it take?

I needed to tell someone. Yes, I know I couldn't tell another living soul for as long as I lived about my heinous crimes, but there was nothing wrong with telling the dead. My head felt like a lead weight as the fatigue began to weigh heavily on me, but my need to share the darkest secret of my life trumped everything else.

Heading back out to the car, I looked up into the sky and felt more alive than ever before. The clear blue sky stretched as far as the eye could see. A slight breeze brushed the very tops of the trees in silence, offering a bit of a reprieve from the midday sun, but then again, I enjoyed the heat I always had. So did my grandma, and it was her who I intended to share my story with.

In the years following her death, I'd made it my mission to visit her every Sunday at noon on the dot. It was the very same time of the week when we used to catch up for a chat during my school years, and after her passing, it just kind of became a tradition for me. Eventually, the little ritual became biweekly when I had more downtime, and soon after, it changed to every so often. I still visited her grave on occasion, but nowhere near as often as I would have liked.

Los Angeles Garden Cemetery was where her mother lay resting, having passed some forty years earlier. She often spoke about wanting to rest next to her and made me swear to bury her in the spot upon her death. I grabbed a fresh bunch of lilies on my way through the gate and felt a little pinch of shame when I placed them on the stained lid of her plot.

"I'm so sorry for neglecting you, Gran," I whispered as I kneeled beside her headstone and went to work cleaning it as best I could with my sleeve.

It wasn't as bad as I thought, and after a little bit of water from my bottle, I managed to shine up the marble lid to a respectable level. Once done, I sat down cross-legged and stared at her name on the headstone.

"I hope you've been enjoying the sunshine," I told her as I looked around; I wanted to make sure there was nobody close enough to listen. Once I was absolutely sure we were alone, I lowered my voice and let out my secret.

Although I believe in God and understand that to Him, a sin is a sin, I felt a strong obligation to help those who can't help themselves. I'll seek forgiveness when the time is right. In reality, every time is the right time, but for my unknown future, I feel the need to protect. So, as I sat in that cemetery explaining to a woman who passed away ten years ago that I had begun hunting down domestic abusers and dealing with them through tragic accidents. I knew it wasn't the proper resolution, but it sure did halt the suffering.

I got quite a bit emotional at one point; a few tears fell after I mentioned how much I loved my job at the hospital, helping everyone who came through the door. I guess telling her about my accomplishments just touched a nerve with me. Anyway, I've been shielding myself since her death. It shouldn't have surprised me, given the amount of grieving I went through over the years. With no other family, she was the last in the world I hated to see leave. Although the Bible says the spirit will return to God who gave it, and I know she's not here, but talking to something makes you feel like you're talking to someone.

It was only when I left the cemetery a couple of hours later that I realized I was on a roll. No matter if it's termed fate, a calling, or an illusion of destiny, even though I may not align with God's views, I'm doing my best to stop instances of brutality from unfolding. And if I had more work to complete, then I would be more than ready to oblige.

What I wanted most during my drive home was to get to my apartment and fall into bed. The tiredness felt overwhelming, and I think I could have slept until the following morning, but unfortunately for me, Peg had other ideas. She sent me a message asking if I had any plans for that night, and I waited until I got back to my apartment to answer her.

Just a decent night's sleep, was what I sent back, and she replied with the laughing emoji, the one with the tears spilling from the eyes and the face tilted slightly to the left. A few seconds later, another text came through, this one asking whether I wanted to join her and Mackenzie for a girls' night out in nearby Midland. Peg's sister was celebrating her birthday at JJ's, one of the more popular clubs in the area that she part-owned.

Sleep was what I wanted at that moment, but I also craved some loud music and dancing, something I hadn't done in far too long. There was just something about letting one's hair down once in a while that helped balance the whole adulting thing we'd been brainwashed into thinking we had to do.

OK, count me in, I texted her, and she sent back a smiley face followed by telling me that she would pick me up around eight.

Eight was perfect. Not only did it give me plenty of time to get myself ready, but I would also sneak in a few hours of much-needed sleep before then. I bounded up the stairs to my second-floor apartment and once inside, dropped my handbag by the door, kicked my shoes off nearby, and fell into bed like a zombie. I must have been out in like seconds because the next thing I knew, my phone began vibrating somewhere near my chin, and when I reached for it and checked the screen,

Peg was asking whether she needed to pick me up anything before everyone took off to the club.

I didn't need anything, but still tired because I'd slept in yet again. A part of me wondered whether it had anything to do with my extracurricular activities since I hadn't slept in for anything since like grade school. Feeling like my eyelids weren't my own, I forced them open as I dragged my butt out of bed and hurried to jump in the shower.

If there was one thing I hung onto from my youth, it was the belief that the only single outfit in the world that was acceptable to be worn to a nightclub was the proverbial little black dress. I had several in my closet, and I instinctively grabbed the first thing my fingers touched. Half an hour later, and with my make-up almost applied, a knock on the door pulled me from my distracted thoughts.

I'd been thinking about the accident from earlier that morning and wondering whether any official reports had been released yet. Thanks to me stupidly sleeping in, I didn't get a chance to check the news, and so here I was, headed out into the night, still oblivious as to the cause of Ben Traiforos's so-called accident.

"Hey, look at you, sexy lady,' Peg said when I opened the door for her. Mackenzie stood behind her, and Brianna, a trainee working in the hospital's nursery, stood behind her. Each of them gave me a hug on the way past, except for

Mackenzie, who planted a kiss on my cheek. "About time you agreed to come hang out with your crew," Peg said once we were in the living room.

"Yeah, well, may as well enjoy myself while I still can," I said and continued through to the bathroom to finish the rest of my make-up.

The four of us piled into Mackenzie's Corolla half an hour later, with Peg and me taking the backseat. The truth is, I wanted to let my hair down for once, and not just a little bit. After working three days a week at the hospital with the occasional four, some nights were endless, and other times gave you a surprise during those 12 hour shifts. But lately, my new hobby has started to revolve around extracurricular activities.

What I wanted to do was cut loose and party like I used to back in my college years, when life just felt like an open book. Although it may have seemed like I had transformed into a kind of guardian angel, the truth was it still didn't feel like it was my life I was living. If anything, I felt a sort of imposter syndrome to the whole savior thing. Maybe I wasn't the one fate intended to send, but I somehow ended up with the job because of some stupid mistake.

Halfway to the nightclub, Peg asked Mackenzie to pull into a gas station so she could use the bathroom, and while the two of them went inside, I remained in the car with Brianna.

I pulled out my phone while waiting and scanned a couple of the news websites for anything about that morning's accident. While the medical report still hadn't been released, I did find a brief video someone had taken of Sophia Traiforos walking out of the hospital.

A chill ran through me when I saw how devastated she looked. Not just devasted but downright distraught. The camera zoomed in enough for me to see her bloodshot eyes, the kind of eyes that had suffered through traumatic sobbing for who knows how long. Seeing her in that condition shook me to the bone because it was the first time I questioned whether I had actually done the right thing.

Who knew how the husband and his wife met each other? That was the first time I really thought about them as a couple, a couple who may have been together since high school. For all I knew, they could have been childhood sweethearts and had been supporting each other forever. That was when I watched the camera skim across the tops of her forearms and saw a hint of the bruises I'd seen firsthand back when I examined her. The bruises, painful marks upon marks left by an abuser who tormented her very existence.

"Who's that," Peg suddenly said from beside me, and I flinched in surprise, having not heard them climb back into the car.

"It's the wife of that man who died on the highway this morning."

"Ewww," Brianna said from the front seat. "I drove past that and saw it. So disgusting."

"That bad, huh," Peg asked.

"It was really gross. Definitely not something you want to see."

"Someone said he jumped out of his truck and was clutching his chest," Peg said. "Didn't see the other traffic and boom, snuffed out, just like that."

"Was he having a heart attack," I asked.

"Not sure," Peg said. "Anyway, I don't want to talk about some old guy dying. We got a party to go to."

While I did put my phone away, I couldn't say the same for my brain, which began to roll the new information over. Clutching his chest... possibly a heart attack...but what about the spiked donut someone tried to kill him with? It didn't make sense to me, and not making sense proved to be an unwanted distraction for me.

When we reached the nightclub and parked the car, I silently forced myself to push Ben Traiforos from my mind and focus on the night. I'd had enough of killings and deaths and abused women, and all I wanted was to forget, even if it was for just one night.

Inside, Peg pulled us over to where her sister Ellie stood talking to a group of guys. She gave each of us a hug and called one of the bartenders over with a stamp, which he used to mark each of our wrists.

"Free drinks for you ladies tonight," Ellie insisted, and who were we to argue?

The inside of JJ's proved to be popular with people practically packing the place out. A narrow stage wrapped around the entire perimeter of the main dance floor, and bikini-clad ladies stood every dozen feet or so dancing to the music. A second-floor balcony hung above it, and people sat inside discreet booths with curtains drawn across the back of them for added privacy. A wall of windows flowed above the dancing platform so people could watch the main arena.

Up on the main stage, a female DJ worked the crowd as the beat of the music echoed across the room. The bulk of the people bounced in perfect rhythm as the dance floor appeared to breathe, almost alive with activity. It drew me in so easily, and within seconds of stepping onto the floor, I found myself dancing along with dozens of people. The sheer volume practically swallowed me up as we became one.

I lost track of time as my body felt detached from the rest of me, the vibrations of the music reaching my inner soul through the floor. The beat rocked the air with echoes while the rhythm shook my insides, my feet and arms moving in a way I hadn't felt in years. It was only when I heard some screaming threats somewhere nearby that I and the rest of those lost in the music found ourselves pulled back into the present.

"I SAID NOW," this guy was yelling into the face of a girl, his fingers firmly wrapped around her neck. Another guy standing close by reached over to pull his friend back but found himself shoved away.

"DON'T TOUCH ME," he shouted at this guy, trying to stop whatever was happening. He turned back to the girl, who looked more scared than a child. "NOW!"

The music continued to beat over the top of the argument, and while most of the people quickly resumed their dancing, I wasn't one of them. Something inside me stirred as I watched the girl get dragged off the dance floor. I pretended to gyrate a bit to blend in with the crowd, but I did so while slowly moving toward where the guy shoved his girlfriend into one of the booths.

I don't know whether it was intuition or maybe something deeper, but an eerie kind of tingling ran down my spine as I watched the couple for several minutes. It was evident that he liked to control her, and given how little she retaliated, I could see this wasn't even the half of it. If this was how he treated her in public, I couldn't begin to imagine what would happen behind closed doors.

I wasn't sure what exactly it was I was waiting for, but when the girl eventually got up and headed alone to the women's bathroom, I knew my moment had come. It was in that exact instant that it wasn't some random nightclub I had been brought to. This had been fate's plan all along.

Making my way into the ladies' bathroom, I found close to a dozen women lined up near the cubicles while more stood in front of the mirrors three deep. A couple of girls near the front were in the middle of snorting lines of white powder, the rest were busy reapplying their make-up. The only person of interest to me stood near the front next to one of the girls snorting, and I could tell she was pissed.

Faking bad make-up, I grabbed my own pieces out of my purse and joined the back of the line, doing my best to try and listen in on the conversation. There was more than one going on, which made listening to that specific one all the more difficult.

"Why do you put up with it, girl," her friend asked when she came up for air and began rubbing the sides of her nose. "Rob already wants to beat the crap out of him after I told him what he did to you."

"He promised me he was going to get some help," the other girl said.

"Oh, yeah, right. And how many times has he said that now?" She leaned into her friend and pulled her a little closer.

"Three years, and he still smacks you around like trash." The other girl looked shyly around. "Well, it's true. He's going to end up killing you; I can see it." That was when one of the other girls spoke up.

"Man, if my guy ever dared lay a hand on me, he'd better have three more behind it. Ain't no way he'd survive long enough to use them."

"Girl, mind your own business," the other one snapped defensively. "This doesn't concern you."

"Geez, sorry," the girl said and decided it best to get out of there.

Despite doing her best to try and help, I could see that the girl, who I learned was named Zoey, was just trying to do her best.

This lady who I was observing wasn't going to leave her abusive boyfriend. Maybe she loved him and believed him to be her soulmate. Up until that moment, I still wasn't entirely sure my services were warranted, but that was when the girl dropped her phone, and when she bent down to pick it up, I saw enough bruises on her back that immediately reminded me of Sophia Traiforos.

What I saw through the gap in the crowd was a section of her back covered in the familiar purplish stain flanked by aged yellow healing. Bruises on bruises was what I called them, and my insides just about knotted when I thought about the piece of shit who had grabbed her in the middle of the dance floor without a single care about who saw him do it. An arrogant, dreadful bastard who saw women as property, and no amount of therapy would remedy that. The only remedy to properly fix that dill hole was the kind I dealt, vengeance.

Chapter 11

Finding the girl after that night turned out to be quite an effort in itself. With me not having a car and being unable to simply excuse myself from the party, I had no way of following the girl home. What I ended up doing was coming up with an on-the-spur idea, to at least get a name.

I ran into her friend again near the bar a short time later, and that was when I dropped a simple fishing hook.

"Hi, I saw you talking to a friend in the bathroom earlier who I think I used to go to school with. Her name is Maggie, right? Maggie Price?"

"Ah, no," she said, giving me an up-and-down look that didn't surprise me. I might have been pushing the similar age thing a little too far. "Her name is Heather Martin."

"Oh, I could have sworn it was my friend. Anyway, sorry," I said, and after offering a weak smile, I headed off to find Peg and the girls.

It was weak, I know, but it did work and gave me perhaps one of the only clues I could have gotten, given the circumstances. To make sure I wouldn't forget it, I sent the name to myself in a text, and when I received it, something new struck me. What if someone eventually did find out what I'd been up to?

The thing is, even some of the most innovative, well-thought-out crimes came unstuck because of the smallest mistakes and tiny oversights the perpetrators missed while planning them. The masterminds of our greatest crimes are only known because they got caught. Was I really above all of them, and would I continue this indefinitely?

While the rest of the night went by without any more interruptions, I couldn't quite get back into the same frame of mind that I had before the argument. The vibe was just gone, and I ended up spending the final couple of hours sitting at a table with the rest of the girls, watching Peg talk with her sister. It was almost 2 am when Mackenzie called it quits and told everyone it was time to go home since she had a morning shift starting in just four hours.

Peg remained with her sister while the rest of us made our way back to Odessa. Mackenzie dropped me off first, and after giving me a final hug, I headed back to my apartment. I walked through the door but felt like I needed a decent sleep, having had my previous one cut short. With Heather Martin's name safely stored in my phone messages, I went to bed knowing I would have work to do when I eventually woke up again, work that I was actually looking forward to.

Perhaps due to a few drinks in my system, I slept like a log for eight straight hours and didn't wake again until after eleven. I didn't think I partied too much, but the pulsing through my head told me otherwise. Anytime you spend too much time at a concert or a club there's a chance your head is still pounding from the decibels. I groaned as I sat up, my mouth uncomfortably dry. Killing two birds with one stone, I pushed through the discomfort and headed to the kitchen to make some coffee and breakfast.

I did pop a couple of painkillers when I took my first sip of coffee some ten minutes later; hopefully, this headache would slowly dissipate. I began with the morning's news, slowly sipping my coffee as I scrolled through several sites. I started with the international news, trying to get a handle on how our fine world was progressing through another day. But this morning, I also wanted everything I could find on a specific fatal accident that had occurred during the previous morning's rush.

Something about seeing the story the first time stirred my insides.

The initial site's headline read Early Morning Tragedy Brings Traffic to Standstill, and I read the entire article twice before moving on to the second site and then the third. None of them offered anything new regarding Ben Traiforos's reasons for jumping out of his truck. Still, I had an idea that he might have taken a nibble of a particular donut, found it to be difficult to swallow, and ended up jumping out to heave up his breakfast.

The sites did name him and mentioned the victim leaving behind a wife and two sons, but to me, the only real victim of this unfortunate accident was the poor truck driver who turned the domestic abuser into pulp. It was he who might end up suffering and seeking some therapy. But it wasn't anything I could change, so I pushed the thought aside. I focused on knowing that Sophia Traiforos had finally been relieved from her abuser.

Once I was sure there wasn't anything else to find out about the accident, I took another sip of coffee and opened up my Instagram app, the first step in trying to find yet another victim who I knew would need help. After scrolling through all the accounts and not finding the one face I remembered from earlier that morning, I switched over to Facebook to see if I had better results. Not only did I find the same girl staring back at me from one of the profile pictures near the top of the search results, but I also found her linked to the psycho who had no issues grabbing a defenseless girl by the throat in front of dozens of party animals.

The thing I loved more than anything about social media was the sheer lack of common sense when it came to people posting their entire lives on these platforms, especially those seeking attention. Kane Nazif was just that type of person. In many of his pictures, he could be seen gazing into a mirror while holding his phone in front of him, capturing a variety of angles of his physique. Yes, he might have had an alright body, but the sheer arrogance in his expression was an instant turn-off for me, as well as knowing just how much of an asshole he was.

Out of his 7,438 followers, 99% of them turned out to be young women all suffering from the same need for attention, the majority of their feeds filled with nothing more than bikini shots, although a lot couldn't even be classed as clothing. The tiniest bits of material covered those spots, with hundreds, if not thousands, of likes for each image.

I went through his friend's list and checked out a few guys he had on there. I found one with the same surname, although that guy appeared to be a few years older. The rest shared one commonality between them, a car club they all belonged to, some MOPAR group where they shared a passion for modifying junkers.

Going back through Heather Martin's page, I scrolled through a couple of years of posts, looking for more about the girl's past. From what I could tell, it looked as if she and

Kane had only been going out for about six months, and in every photo of the couple she posted, he always had one hand holding the back of her neck. Some of her friends left comments about the two, and while some approved, I did find a couple that mentioned that he needed a chill pill.

One girl in particular, named Paisley, left comments attacking Kane with accusations of control and narcissism. Several of her comments had angry-face emojis next to them and when I looked closer, those emojis had been left by Heather. I think I knew why she left them, knowing how fiery her boyfriend was.

The other thing I noticed which kind of threw me at first was the number of comments to photos that never showed up no matter how many times I tried showing All Comments. Facebook had an option under posts where a person could arrange comments based on the Newest, Most Relevant, or All. I tried selecting All several times for a number of her posts, and the numbers just never added up. That was until I finally figured out why.

She was hiding them. Not deleting them but manually hiding them, going into each post to make sure they wouldn't be seen by her boyfriend but also not showing as deleted by the original poster.

I wondered just how many comments she'd hidden in her time with Kane to save herself from a beating, how many times she'd felt the need to protect herself while trying not to offend her friends.

When I reached about as far down the page as I wanted to go, I began scrolling back up, going over old ground as I rolled the information around in my head. I randomly paused on a post from a couple of months earlier that showed Heather Martin sitting alone at a table with a birthday cake in front of her. At that moment, I happened to come across a tipping point for me. Was fate yet again guiding me or simply watching to see where I would end up?

Something about the photo caught my attention. I think it was the expression on her face that didn't quite suit the moment, a kind of sadness hanging behind the forced smile. I clicked on the post to check out some of the comments, and it was apparent that several others had noticed what I had seen. Most of the comments wished the girl a happy birthday, as one might expect but several of them didn't wish her an amazing day per se. Instead, they wrote that they hoped her day would get better, hinting at some event that might have thrown her celebration off course.

None of the people commenting gave any indication as to what the issue might have been, although I did find one single person who dropped a huge hint. This could be Melinda Bryant all over again, was what the person had written, but nobody else had left a reaction to the comment or replied to it. It was a complete surprise to me, given what I ended up finding out.

Melinda Bryant wasn't a name I remembered seeing during my scrolling through the bunch of friends associated with either person. I expanded my search to the entire platform, but those who I found didn't seem to have any direction connection to either Heather Martin or Kane Nazif. When Facebook wasn't helping me, I took my search over to Instagram, but that also didn't do any assistance. I spent a good twenty minutes hunting through both platforms, but it proved that it wasn't time well spent.

Feeling frustrated, I ended the session, took my cup over to the sink, and gave it a rinse before placing it down in the dishwasher. The sun streaming in through the open window looked way too good to pass up, and after drying my hands, I headed to the bedroom and swapped the sweat pants for tights, the t-shirt for a crop top, slipped into some sneakers, grabbed one of my baseball caps, and headed out for a run.

I love running. To me, running is one of those activities that traverses more than just one need. It's a simple exercise that's perfect for fitness, health, boredom, socializing in a roundabout way, and thinking. In fact, thinking while running has become my favorite way to clear my mind and explore new ideas on whatever route I choose.

I'd say I was pretty fit. It's not that I've ever run a marathon or anything, but I managed a few miles at a time if I really put my mind to it. The reason for the run was what mattered, and the more complicated the problem, the longer I found myself running. Trying to figure out if a random stranger warranted me coming after her abusive boyfriend proved to be one of those issues that kept me pounding the pavement for a lot longer than I planned.

I must have covered at least four miles before I realized that I was beaten, four miles along several city blocks until my obnoxiously fast breathing finally pulled me back into the moment. Or maybe it was one of the jets taking off from the airport, roaring into the sky, flashing its lights on the sides of the wings above my head, that caught my attention. In any case, it was while watching that jet continue to rise into the air that I suddenly had a thought. Two, in fact. The first was that I needed to get my shit together if I was going to take this gig seriously. The second was that I had an idea about how to find out who Melinda Bryant was.

Chapter 12

Murder. That was the first thing that came to mind when I finally found out the meaning behind the name Melinda Bryant. It wasn't any social media platform that helped me learn the story behind it; instead, I did a simple Google search when I returned home from buying my new laptop and cell phone. As it turned out, Melinda was Kane Nazif's ex-girlfriend. The very first hit from the search landed me on an old news article from two years earlier.

Melinda had been reported missing by her sister, who had grown increasingly worried for her welfare. After receiving a phone call from her earlier in the week, the sister sensed that something was off. The conversation had been filled with distress, and her sister's voice trembled as she spoke about feeling overwhelmed and anxious. Days passed without any contact, and the sister's concern deepened. She tried calling multiple times, but each attempt ended with silence.

Frantic and unable to shake the feeling that something was seriously wrong, she decided to report her sister missing, hoping that authorities could help find her and bring her home safely. According to the sister, Melinda had been fighting with her boyfriend over his repeated cheating and being pregnant with their first child; it wasn't just some random boy. After promising to come over to her house, the sister notified the police late the following afternoon that her sister never made it over.

It took law enforcement almost a week to find Melinda in an abandoned vehicle. All later reports indicated that the expectant mother took her own life. Although Nazif was taken into custody in the initial phases of the investigation, he was ultimately released without any concrete charges. Despite Melinda's family insisting there was no way the girl would have taken her own life, a lack of evidence ensured Kane Nazif's release.

Looking into the story a little more, I ended up finding subsequent articles and social media posts showing the boyfriend taking little time to mourn the deaths of his girlfriend and unborn son, finding himself a new girl just a week after their funeral. The photos of him I saw posted showed someone without the slightest hint of grief.

One photo in particular on a friend's Instagram rubbed me up the wrong way, an image that had been uploaded the very day of the funeral. It showed Kane sitting in between several of his buddies in some bar, each with a bottle of suds in their hands and wearing the biggest grins. One of the comments posted alongside the photo said, "Nothing better than freedom."

I'm not sure how long I sat on the couch staring at that photo; the burning desire to slap the grin from his face was growing hotter by the second. It was guys like Kane Nazif who enjoyed torturing anyone weaker than them, feeding off their suffering like sadistic leeches. I must find him. I needed to use my newfound purpose in life and remove him from the lives of anybody dumb enough to consider him a partner. I needed to save Heather Martin before she ended up like Melinda Bryant!

Along with setting up the new laptop with the VPN, I successfully downloaded the TinEye software, which can analyze any image and find its location by searching for similar images. Several of Heather Martin's posts showed her inside a gym that she seemed to frequently visit. After running a few of the images through the software, I found out it was at The Fitness Center in West Odessa.

What the photo didn't give me was time, but when checking each of the posts, I saw all uploaded between four and six in the afternoon. It took me barely seconds to make up my mind. After packing some essentials into a bag, I jumped in my car and headed to my first proper stakeout. I have a two-hour window waiting around, but this time I have snacks!

With the gym sitting on one of the corners of a busy intersection and a parking lot filled to near capacity, it became apparent that trying to stay in the car and monitor all traffic would be next to impossible. I quickly changed tactics. Instead of remaining in the car and risking missing the woman, I decided to head inside and pretend that I needed some training. With my new membership and being able to use any of the seven locations spread across the greater Odessa area, I might as well take advantage of this opportunity.

Hardly anyone paid me the slightest attention when I walked around, carrying nothing but a water bottle and car keys. It's a good sign that people are there for personal transformations and to get their crunk on. I would have typically had a towel but forgot to pack one for this contingency, and thankfully, none of the staff walked around bothering people.

One of the rooms had an aerobics class, while the other room had a boxing class. The free-weights area looked about the busiest of all, but I ignored them all and headed straight to the back of the room, where rows of exercise bikes stood in a two-deep line. I jumped on one away from a couple of other riders, made sure I popped my earbuds in and slowly began to get into a rhythm. With no way of knowing how long I'd be sitting on the bike, I knew I had to pace myself.

For the first thirty minutes, I wasn't sure whether I had any chance of spotting the one person amongst a hundred sweaty bodies all moving about. The busiest seemed to be just after the end of one of the classes and before the next one began, but it was exactly at that time that I spotted Heather Martin walking out of the aerobics session. It was the fiercely bright pink t-shirt she wore that caught my eye; I had her clearly in view; there was no way I was letting her slip away.

She spent the first few minutes in a conversation with a couple of girls before turning to the locker rooms. I assumed she'd take a shower and freshen up. It took almost another half hour before she emerged again, and when she did, she had a bag slung over her shoulder and a bottle of water in her hand.

It was a bit of a touch-and-go situation between the moment she left the gym and me trying to follow her. Without knowing which car was hers, I couldn't run back to mine, and with the parking lot having two exits, it was a toss-up between whether she would take the one closer to my car or not. I shouldn't have doubted fate stepping in to help. Not only did she jump into her black Rav-4 near the closest exit to where I parked, but she also sat in the car doing her make-up long enough for me to get to mine before she rolled out onto the road.

The next hour was spent following her to a couple of stores before she finally headed down a suburban street and pulled into the driveway of a house on West 15th Street. From the way she parked her car, to the way she checked the mailbox, unlocked the door, and casually walked inside, I could tell this was her house, and I settled in for however long it would take me to learn more. It wasn't Heather I was seeking, after all, but her boyfriend.

I parked my car a few houses away, giving me a clear view of her home. As I waited, I occupied myself eating some pistachio nuts, keeping an eye on what was happening. Traffic along the street wasn't too bad, with vehicles passing by maybe every five minutes or so. Each time I saw one approach, my heart beat elevated in anticipation of it either pulling up in front of the house or turning into the driveway parking behind the Rav.

Peg phoned me around seven for a general chat, and it was a welcome distraction from the increasing pressure on my bladder. I ensured not to drink too much to avoid such a situation, but then stupidly ate more than a few salted nuts, which kind of worked against me. She was busy telling me about how she ended up staying at the club a little longer than expected, and she slept at her sister's house until lunchtime. Eventually had a BLT sandwich before her sister drove her back home.

I was considering asking her if I could take a week off when a Dodge Ram suddenly slowed down near my car, which startled me a little bit as I held my breath. The windows were dark, and I couldn't quite see inside the cabin from my angle, but it continued toward Heather's house before stopping directly in front.

"Eliza, are you OK? What were you saying?"

"Sorry, never mind," I said, remembering that changing my routine could potentially throw up red flags to anybody investigating the case...if there was a case. "Hey, listen, I gotta go. You'll be at work tomorrow, right?"

"Yeah, sure. I'll see you there?"

"Definitely," I said.

"Are you sure everything's OK?"

"Yes, I'm fine," I was hoping that I hadn't thrown off any suspicious behavior.

"Alright, just making sure."

"See you tomorrow."

I ended the call and immediately pressed the lock button to darken the screen again as I watched the man of the moment briefly walk into the house and subsequently disappear as the door shut. Another set of headlights approached from further down the streets and briefly lit up my car's interior, but I managed to slide down enough to keep from being seen.

I know it wasn't too dark outside, but in another 30 minutes, it soon will.

Not knowing whether Kane would stay for the night, I checked my watch and made a mental note that I'd wait till midnight and then take off. I figured that, with the lack of fluid intake, I might be able to cross my legs until then, but that might stretch my bladder control to the limit. I wanted to Google how people on stakeouts dealt with bodily functions but didn't want to light up my phone again, so I decided against it.

An hour after Kane turned up, a low growling began to fill the cabin of my car as hunger set in. I considered my Snickers bar that I had packed, but just as I reached for it, shouting suddenly erupted out on the street, and when I looked up, I saw Kane standing on Heather's porch, shouting something through the open front door. Everyone in the neighborhood could have seen the explosive anger on his face as he screamed something incomprehensible at his girlfriend. When he walked down the couple of steps and turned back to follow up his initial tirade with another, I saw Heather appear in the doorway.

What Kane projected with rage, Heather reflected back at him with fear, the two of them, the chalk and cheese of relationships.

What struck me was how Kane seemed to revel in her vulnerability; the girl's frail demeanor seemed to fuel his narcissism. At that moment, he could have easily walked away, turned around, and gotten into his truck. I still had my window cracked and thought about rolling it down, but doing so might involve someone noticing motion in the vehicle, which could give away my presence to either one. I decided against it, figuring it was best to keep my eavesdropping to a minimum.

Kane did walk back up the stairs toward Heather. Just like I'd seen him do back at the nightclub, he lunged at her with an outstretched hand, his fingers closing around her neck. Heather didn't react as I had anticipated; I attributed that to her awareness of the inevitable escape. He pulled her in close, almost spitting more abuse into her face in a display fueling my anger. It was at that very point I knew what had to be done if I wanted Heather Martin to avoid becoming another Melinda Bryant.

If it hadn't been for some stranger yelling at the couple from across the street, who knows how far the argument would have continued? Kane took the hint. He let Heather go, gave her a sharp push to the chest, and walked back to his truck. I waited until he'd driven a good block up the road before starting up my car and commencing the pursuit.

The fuel burning inside me felt much hotter than either of the previous men I'd taken care of. If anyone ever needed a guardian angel to intervene, it would be for Heather Martin.

Chapter 13

Kane Nazif was a man who knew what he had, a man who didn't mind flashing his pearly whites and good looks to get into the panties of unsuspecting women. His first stop after leaving Heather's was a bar downtown, where I watched him emerge onto an outdoor deck where he met a couple of friends. He'd barely sat down before three girls walked past, and he pulled one onto his lap where she resisted at first but where she remained.

When he grew tired of that, Kane fist-bumped with each of his friends, stuck his tongue down the random girl one last time, and headed back to his truck. Just before he climbed in, I watched him pause long enough to stare at his phone screen for a bit, typed some sort of message, and then took off with a specific destination in mind.

I thought he might have been exchanging messages with his girl and would head back to Heather's, something I definitely hoped he wouldn't do, but for once, I was happy he proved me wrong. We drove back the same way we came but a mile from his girlfriend's turn-off. Kane turned down another random street, drove for three blocks, and pulled over to the side of the road. A second later, someone stepped out of the shadows, leaned in through the window, and remained there for a few seconds. It was only when I saw the person reach into their pocket and hand something over that I realized, Kane was buying drugs.

To save the location, I pulled out my phone and bookmarked the spot in my Map app before continuing on tailing Kane's truck when he took off again. Half a dozen blocks further up, he pulled into a new driveway and turned the truck off. This time, when he stepped onto the porch, a different girl walked out of the house to greet him, and judging by the way she hung off his neck and clamped onto his lips, this wasn't the first time he'd visited.

They disappeared into the house, and I decided to hang around and see just how long this little visit would last. I figured that if Kane hadn't emerged after a couple of hours, then I could go home and pick up my little stalking mission the following day or at another time. I was just beginning to settle in after the first hour when he suddenly emerged again, this time the girl wrapped up in a bed sheet as she gave him a longing kiss while leaning against the doorframe.

Seeing him in the arms of another woman only served to add to my conviction, and it also caused me to wonder how many more women he had around town. Being a player was one thing, but the thought that someone wielding his kind of volatility and was actively farming multiple causal relationships could only serve to further spread violence and fear.

With his night still not over, I followed Kane for another drive through the next city until he pulled into a familiar place, the parking lot of the nightclub where I first saw him half-strangle his girlfriend. It was at that point, watching as he climbed out of his truck and made his way inside, that I decided I'd seen enough. Whatever else he had planned for his night would be his own to enjoy.

With my mind made up that Kane Nazif would indeed be the third domestic abuser I would remove from this world. I headed home, where I'd eventually lay down with a thousand thoughts running through my mind. That night, I expected to dream about all the vile and disgusting things this latest monster did to his victims, especially after having spent so long following him, but instead, I found myself dreaming of absolutely nothing.

When I woke up the following morning just a few minutes before noon, I was almost surprised by just how relaxed I felt. Deep sleep wasn't really a thing for me, not someone with an overactive brain that, at times, refused to shut down. In any case, I climbed out of bed feeling a lot better than I expected and started my day off with a long shower and an even longer coffee out on my balcony, scrolling my phone.

The news sites were my first stop, although I failed to find any mention of Ben Traiforos. That morning tragedy sure brought traffic to a halt. I thought there might have been a follow-up report of some kind, but it appeared as if interest in the story had diminished down to nothing, and the world had simply moved on. I, for one, didn't mind; sometimes in life, you surprise yourself.

These days, whenever I have work, I have decided to make it my mission to have a proper meal with me. Nightshift was tough enough already without me adding to my body's suffering by not giving it enough nutrition. Having no preset meal times during our shift made it difficult to get food when either on the run, between patients, or with nothing but vending machines to use.

Cooking had never really been my thing either, but I found it almost holistic to spend a couple of hours in the kitchen before a stretch of shifts and prepare several nights of meals that I would keep in the freezer. I blasted music while doing so, letting my brain run free during an early afternoon of perfect distraction.

I arrived at work some twenty minutes before the start of my shift with one container of chili con carne and another of steamed rice in my bag, together with an apple and a bag of potato chips. Not exactly three square meals for a twelve-hour shift, I know, but it's definitely an improvement compared to what I was accustomed to before the change.

From the moment I walked into the ED, I felt myself swept into a torrent of activity, almost like falling into the churning waters of a swollen river. Peg grabbed me by the arm and directed me to a 7-year-old's broken collarbone while she headed over to help an elderly patient who'd fallen while gardening.

For the next nine hours, I barely got the chance to breathe, let alone think about anything other than treating people. Of course, Kane remained way back in the shadows of my mind, but he felt far from the focus of my evening. The sheer number of patients walking through the door felt almost overwhelming compared to a regular day, and it wasn't even a full moon.

I typically don't find it necessary to detail the specifics of my shift, especially since you can likely envision the situations I encounter regularly. However, there was one particular incident that stands out. It occurred around four that morning during an event that ultimately provided me with an answer to a question I hadn't yet realized I needed to ask.

One of the ambulances brought in a highly intoxicated woman who sounded just about ready to take on the world with her protesting abusive screams. The two paramedics had struggled to properly strap her onto a stretcher for transport to the ED. She was still fighting to remove the restraints while being wheeled into one of our observational bays by her nurse Roz. The main observation wing held a dozen beds, each separated by nothing more than a curtain, and that's where the first issue occurred.

I could see the repulsion on a couple of the other patients' faces hearing this new arrival carry on, and I did feel sorry for them having to put up with such crap. It indeed increased their stress levels while making everything uncomfortable. An elderly gentleman lying in an adjoining bed, being treated for an irregular heartbeat, was about to receive a shot of Digoxin when the incident happened.

Sitting at the station, I didn't really notice what happened other than hearing it. I had just finished typing my latest patient evaluation and medical management report. When this intoxicated woman gave out one almighty scream, pulled one arm free from the restraints, and started rocking side to side, coming close to rolling off the stretcher. Mr. Farmer's nurse, Harley, was about to give him an injection when she was pushed from behind and had to steady herself to avoid falling. I ran over and just about lost my shit at the woman, grabbing her attention with a tone that would have made any army drill sergeant proud.

"THAT IS ENOUGH," I just about screamed as I smacked my fist against the railing of her bed. The woman froze, her mouth half-hanging open with surprise.

"LIE THERE AND BE QUIET. THE DOCTOR WILL SEE YOU WHEN HE'S READY."

For a second, I thought she was going to come back at me with some renewed aggression, but surprisingly, the woman snapped her mouth closed and carefully edged her way back to the middle of the stretcher. I held my gaze on her, and when she slowly calmed down and stared at the ceiling, I knew I'd pulled off the impossible.

I walked around the curtain to where Roz stood, looking down at the tiniest trail of blood running down her forearm. "Oh Roz, you're bleeding," are the words that drew my attention away from the intoxicated woman. When Harley was nudged trying to give the atrial fibrillation patient his injection, she accidentally poked Roz on the other side of the curtain.

Roz said, "I didn't even notice," as she walked over to the sink and grabbed some paper towels.

Harley ended up disposing of the first syringe and replacing it with another, but that minor mishap didn't go unnoticed by me. Call it a lightbulb moment, if you will, because that small scene was enough to send electricity through my head, the epiphany feeling more like an eye-opening bolt of lightning. I suddenly knew exactly how I could get Kane Nazif.

Thankfully, nobody noticed how distracted I became for the rest of that shift, and I don't think I could have held in my excitement any longer than I did.

"How did I not think of this sooner?" I asked myself as I climbed into my car early that morning, ignoring the sunrise for perhaps the first time in forever.

I made my first stop at an Aldi for fresh supplies, namely a couple of energy drinks. Not knowing how long the next step in my plan would take, I wanted to make sure I was prepared. I was able to get some cash back at the checkout counter to avoid paying that stupid $3.50 ATM fee. Am I the only one who thinks it's crazy how banks charge you money to get your own money?

Buying drugs had never been my forte. Actually, I had never bought them on a street level before, so this was an entirely new experience for me. I guess I could have purchased them anywhere, but I figured that if any subsequent investigations did take place, then it would make sense to use the same supplier I knew Kane already used.

The plan I'd conjured up, thanks to seeing that little incident between Harley and Roz, was simple. I was going to buy the same drugs that I saw Kane purchase and deliver him a hit that would take him out. People died from overdoses all the time, and the authorities barely batted an eyelid over them. All I had to do was get my timing right.

I parked half a dozen blocks from the bookmarked spot where I'd seen Kane buy his drugs and settled in to wait. Not knowing whether these people had specific business opening times or a guaranteed roadside spot weren't matters I understood, so I figured I'd sit back and watch for a bit. If I saw cars begin to pull up and someone walked out to offer them curbside service, then I figured I'd try to do the same.

It wasn't long before I saw the first car slow as it turned onto the block before stopping near the same spot as Kane did. When someone walked to the passenger side window, I couldn't quite make out who they were, but from my point of view, I watched as they reached in through the window and grabbed whatever was held out for them before pulling something out of their back pocket.

The entire exchange was over within seconds, and both parties departed the spot just as fast as they had arrived. I watched the car slowly roll toward the next intersection, turn left, and disappear back into the world.

"Just one more," I whispered to myself as I felt a familiar tightening in my stomach. That was the moment I confirmed to myself that I would be one of those people rolling up to buy drugs in the not-too-distant future. I just hoped I could blend in with the rest of the clientele.

Ten minutes later, a second car rolled up, this time something I wasn't expecting. The vehicle wasn't just another junker driven by some poor meth head but instead, a flashy new BMW, the shiny red paint job gleaming in the sunshine. As for the transaction itself, the same process quickly followed. The guy emerged from his usual spot, leaned in through the window, took the cash, and tossed a package inside the cabin before the customer continued with their day. Total transaction time was just thirty seconds from stop to go.

I wanted to wait for a third car just to be sure, but I knew it was only the fear within me trying to delay the inevitable. If I had given in to that overwhelming sense, I don't think I would have gone through with the buy and simply driven home.

"Like ripping off a band-aid," I muttered under my breath as I started the engine, checked my mirrors, and slowly pulled out onto the road.

Halfway down that first block, I pulled some cash from my purse and felt beads of nervous sweat building across my brow. The nerves turned up the beating in my chest as a thousand questions formed in my brain, each one causing me to question what I was about to do. Would the cash I have be enough? Would they think I was an undercover cop? Would they even sell me the drugs? Maybe I didn't look like their usual clientele, and they'd refuse to serve me.

My insides felt like I'd swallowed a boat anchor as I pulled up, one traitorous bead of sweat breaking loose and running down the side of my cheek. I nervously pressed the window button and watched the passenger side roll down, the whirring sound almost mocking me. A shadow moved inside the open door of the house, and within seconds, a guy walked down the steps and came toward me.

Sunglasses hid his eyes, but I could tell he was watching me intently. A slight bulge sat where his jumper met the top of his jeans, and I imagined some form of a pistol tucked into the waistband, a gun he'd use without hesitation if he saw a threat.

He said, "Watcha want," as he grabbed the door and leaned over the car. The only thing I knew of from listening to R&B music rolled off my lips.

I said, "Gimme an 8-Ball," again doubting everything about my presentation, from the money I had in my hand to the look on my face. He considered me for a few seconds, perhaps weighing up whether I was a genuine customer or someone trying to set him up. The moment sure felt like forever, and I could already see him grinning at me before telling me to take a hike.

When I saw his lips begin to part and reveal an intimidating grill running along his teeth, I thought my vision would come true, but instead, he surprised me.

He said, "One hundred," I pulled out five $20 bills and passed them over, which he snatched and counted in a flash.

Once the cash disappeared, I saw the next move in my head, but instead of reaching into the back pocket of his jeans, he went into his jacket. My insides just about flipped as I visualized a gun being pulled out and aimed at me, the error of my ways finally catching up with me. I saw fate flipping me off and actually felt the muscles in my shoulder tense in preparation for grabbing the steering wheel and taking off.

It wasn't a pistol at all. The guy barely flinched as he pulled a clear bag with some white powder from his jacket and dropped it onto the passenger seat beside me. Not bothering with a thank you or a goodbye, he pushed himself off the car, turned, and headed back to the house, leaving me to decide what to do next. I don't think I'd ever felt more urgency to be anywhere else but my present location than I did at that moment.

What I found genuinely amazing while driving to the nearest corner, heading back out into the world like the previous two cars I'd observed, was the way the entire sequence made the rest of existence just disappear. Whether it was the nerves churning in my stomach or my inexperience, I honestly don't believe I noticed anything else in those few seconds I spent parked on that street. People could have come and jacked up my car and stolen my wheels, and I wouldn't have noticed. That was when I had a thought which truly rattled me. What if someone I knew drove past at that very moment and saw me buying drugs?

    I began trembling long before I reached the safety of my apartment, and the first thing I did once inside was grab a glass of water and take large swallows in the hope of regaining control. The fear felt like nothing before, more intense than any confrontation I'd had in living memory. I had just unwittingly risked everything, one brief moment with the potential to bring my entire existence crumbling down around me. In a way, I'd risked my life. If I wanted to thrive in the world I had built for myself, I would have to be much more cautious in the future.

Chapter 14

Research was what I needed to ensure my ongoing survival. No more stupid risks like the one I took buying the drugs. Three glasses of water was what it took for me to finally calm down enough to where I didn't feel incapable of carrying my cell phone over to the couch. The part that worried me was involving someone new in the process of taking care of Kane, namely the guy who sold me the drugs.

What if they somehow traced the lethal dose back to that dealer, and he remembered the girl in the red Civic who made a particular purchase on a specific day and time?

There wasn't anything I could do about the drug dealer, but there were definitely things I could do to ensure I didn't take that kind of risk again. Using my laptop, I began to research as much as possible about the drug I purchased. Yes, I'm a nurse, and yes, I'd treated plenty of people affected by all forms of illicit drugs, but that didn't make me an expert on any of them or their use.

The drugs I had were most likely identical to those purchased by Kane. And if not, well... it's like what the French say: se la vie. Which translates to "that's life" in case you were wondering.

Since it was now in my possession, this was the substance I was going to work with. Although there were other options available, I couldn't take the chance of using a different drug dealer that Kane hadn't tried before. An autopsy would undoubtedly be carried out on him, and a toxicology report issued after his death. How would his friends react to uncovering some crazy, off-the-wall product he'd never been known to use?

Either way, it sure looked like the dealer was selling the same product to everyone.

I planned to inject him in the club while innocently passing by. It was the best and easiest option I could think of, as long as his overdose wouldn't raise suspicions. The thing is, I faced a number of issues, each one only serving to add more questions than answers. If I wanted nothing more than to kill him, then injecting the entire 3.5 grams into him would almost certainly guarantee that. But it could also raise suspicions.

These suspicions might lead law enforcement to search through security footage. That was one thing I definitely needed to avoid. So, if I wanted to avoid raising suspicions, I needed to work out where to inject without raising suspicions. Too little, and I would just be giving him an unexpected high; in the wrong place, I would face unwanted questioning if I was ever caught.

I quickly realized there was one crucial factor that would decide my victory or defeat, so to speak... What it all came down to was giving him a high dosage. Out and about at the nightclub, Kane would probably already be taking something to get his fix. I didn't want to be simply adding to whatever he'd already taken. With 3.5 grams of product equal to 3.5 ml of fluid, as the density of water was 1 gram per ml, this could be easier than I thought.

I wish I could have taken more time to research, but with me on the schedule for that night, I still needed to live my own life. I did hope that Heather would be alright until I could hand deliver my plan for her boyfriend. I'm not sure how I would react if something happened to her before I had my chance to seal the deal.

Unlike the previous shift, where I had the workload to distract me, that night, I spent nearly the majority of my shift thinking about the possible outcomes of killing Kane. Unlike the previous two killings, this one felt a lot closer to home, perhaps because of the way I intended to end him. I still saw Brian Hurst as an accident, possibly one orchestrated by fate, but still an accident. Ben Traiforos, on the other hand, happened at a distance and, in a way, as much of an accident as Hurst before him. It wasn't as if I had personally pushed the man into traffic.

Kane would be different. I'd be right up close beside him, close enough to smell the alcohol on his breath when I stuck him with the needle. Whether he'd feel it was another issue entirely, but one I hoped to avoid by making sure I got him while surrounded by enough people to mask my actions. If he suspected anything while I was close enough, I might find myself at the end of one of his aggressive episodes, and that definitely wouldn't end well.

I think I must have checked the time every five minutes once we passed midnight, each interval feeling more like an hour. With time passing mind-numbingly slow, I tried to keep myself as occupied as possible, which was not an easy task when there weren't enough patients to go around. It was during one of my non-scheduled rounds that Peg sent two of the others home early due to a lack of work, and I kicked myself for missing the opportunity.

The morning did eventually arrive, and when I walked out of the hospital, I swear I could have curled up right there in the back seat of my car and fallen asleep. I was beat, though not from being overworked, that's for sure. Fortunately, I had the weekend free, which provided me ample time to work out the next step in my plan.

One thing that I dreaded when it came to working the night shift was getting home in the morning so damn tired and then finding myself unable to sleep due to a second wind coming on the moment my head touched the pillow. I've had it happen to me a few times over the years, and that morning turned out to be one of those times. I must have tossed and turned for more than an hour before I sat up in bed and stared at the door while contemplating my next move.

I didn't want to get up. What I wanted was to get a few hours of sleep, knowing that once I woke up, I'd be ready to continue with wherever my plan took me. If I didn't take action, I was aware that the exhaustion would come back much worse, disrupting my day at the worst possible moment.

To try and appease both sides, I went out to the living room, grabbed the laptop, and brought it back to the bed, where I lay with a pillow tucked under my chest and began scrolling through a few news sites. When nothing of interest caught my eye, I turned my attention to social media, where I found just what I'd been hoping for within minutes on Facebook.

It was on a post on JJ's nightclub that I found a comment made by Heather Martin. The post wasn't anything specific; it was just a random photo of the dance floor asking who was ready to welcome the weekend. Heather commented, *going to dance up a storm tonight for my man's birthday*, which two others had already liked. Reading the words a second time, a familiar tightening rolled through my belly, a sensation I was beginning to recognize as anticipation.

I did note that neither of the two likes were Kanes, and she hadn't tagged him in the comment. After following a link back to her profile, I also discovered that she hardly ever tagged her boyfriend in her posts. She didn't have as many posts as I would have expected, but I did see the sadness in those eyes within each of her pics. Maybe not precisely unhappiness but more of a fear, one she tried to keep hidden as best she could.

Once I realized that I had finally managed to secure a general time and a place for my planned execution, I thought about the best way of concealing my dark plan. Injecting the drugs into him was already guaranteed, but how would I explain my reason for being there if asked? I couldn't exactly just walk into the place, stab the guy, and then leave again, could I?

That was when I had an idea, one which I hoped would not only cover my intentions but also give me purpose for being there. I clicked into the comment section of JJ's post and typed my own reply, making sure to tag four others. I typed, Hey girls, how about we let our hair down, after I tagged Peg, Mackenzie, Brianna, the trainee, and Darcy Higgins, one of our colleagues who worked as a dedicated phlebotomist in the hospital's dedicated collection center.

Once I was happy with the comment, I pressed the Enter button, waited for the comment to officially post, and closed the laptop. I still felt awake but could sense the fatigue beginning to return and figured I'd try and ride the wave down. No point sitting around waiting for people to see the comment and respond when I had a more pressing issue to deal with...like sleeping.

Maybe because the plan was finally getting some traction, I found myself dozing off almost immediately. Unlike the first time, there was no tossing and turning or frustrated episodes of silence to contend with. This time, I found myself getting caught in that weird space between sleeping and the living world. The dreams that came after simply weren't clear enough to make me believe in their realism.

The great thing was that I didn't need an alarm to wake me, not when I knew I had plenty of time to play with. I wasn't expecting Heather to arrive at the club until after ten, and that was more than enough time for me to prepare.

I always found that waking up naturally always sets the tone for the rest of the day or night for me, and that afternoon proved to be no different. It was just after four that I first heard the horn of a distant truck out on the interstate. Checking my watch, it was the image of Kane and Heather during their previous interaction at JJ's that came to mind, one that drove me to reach over to the nightstand to grab my phone.

Just as I had hoped when I put the phone down several hours before, five Facebook notifications were waiting for me, as well as two text messages. Thankfully, I remembered to switch the phone's Silent mode on before dropping off to sleep. I went into Facebook first and read the comments people had left tagged on my post. Mackenzie, Brianna, and Darcy all agreed to come along for some dancing, while Peg proved to be the odd one out. She didn't reply but instead reacted with a sad emoji. One of the texts turned out to be from her clarifying that she had to work due to one of the others needing time off.

I replied to Peg's text first, then deleted the other, offering me 50% off of a Netflix subscription that I didn't need. Next, I went back to Facebook and responded to each of the girls. After another twenty minutes of scrolling back and forth, Mackenzie offered to drive us there, and I figured it might not be such a bad idea, given my purpose for going in the first place. Mackenzie driving us would give me yet another layer of alibi to hide behind if things didn't go to plan.

Mackenzie offered to pick us all up one by one, and I'll be prepared for a 930 pickup. I'd make sure to get myself ready a lot earlier than that, and not just by dressing myself. To ensure I wouldn't mess up my outfit, or get anything on me, I decided to get dressed last.

I had to make sure the plan was ready to go. I grabbed the powder, distilled water, and the syringe and got busy. From my research, I learned I could mix the cocaine powder with the water, and then all I had to do was put it in the syringe. But safety first, I ensured I was wearing gloves. Apparently, this stuff can just be absorbed into your skin. After everything was mixed really well and prepped, I installed the cap on the needle.

I wish I could have worked out a more foolproof plan than the half-arsed idea that I decided to go with. I knew there were still way too many variables for me to contend with, each one capable of completely derailing my efforts, but with few options. I had to go with what I had. I knew that injecting the drug into the leg muscle and not a vein would mean a much slower release in terms of a high. But it also meant the overdose may not happen immediately, rather once most of the drug had a chance to enter the system.

The more I thought about the process of injecting Kane with the cocaine, the more doubts began to bombard me, and for the last hour, while waiting for Mackenzie to arrive, I put on a movie to distract me. OK, so Jerry Maguire might not have been the best choice, but it did fill the gap with enough soppy romance until I received a text saying, "We are just a couple of minutes away." As soon as I turned off the TV and started gathering my belongings, my nerves surged in waves.

I barely reached the sidewalk outside my building before I saw the Corolla turn into the street. Mackenzie flashed me a wave as she pulled up, as did Darcy, sitting in the passenger seat. I slipped into the backseat beside Brianna, who was already telling me how she pre-gamed a Jack and Coke. After clicking my seatbelt, we were ready to roll out and have a great time.

The girls were so upbeat during the drive to the club, and I wish I could have shared their excitement, but the overwhelming sense of dread refused to let go of me. It wasn't the act itself I was dreading but the possibility of failing. I rechecked Facebook just before we reached the club and came across a post by Heather Martin and again found myself staring into the eyes of a woman locked in a world of fear. There was also a hint of a bruise on the side of her neck that I hadn't noticed before, and the sight of it only served to intensify my nerves. All I wanted to do was get to the club and deliver a new kind of justice.

Chapter 15

When we reached the club's parking lot, it was overwhelming. There was a line that stretched from the main door, and around sixty people were all queued up, waiting to go inside.

"Going to take ages to get inside," Brianna complained beside me before she laid back on the seat rest.

"Won't take long," Mackenzie said as she found a parking spot in the second row. "And besides...Peg gave me her sister's number, so I'll just let her know we've arrived."

"Oh, you little cheat," Brianna said with an evil giggle.

"It's not what you know, sister," Mackenzie said with a hint of attitude and a head tilt. The rest of us laughed at her when she said, "It's who you know!"

Ellie directed us to a side entrance, where she welcomed the four of us in. After a few brief hugs, we followed her inside, the distant doof-doof of serious bass rattling through the place. We walked through a storage area filled with all manner of alcohol and snacks. I followed behind as Ellie led us out to the main foyer.

"Feel free to leave your stuff in my office over there," she said, pointing to one of the doors near the back. She motioned to a security guard stationed at the restricted area and he gave her an acknowledging head nod. "Enjoy your night girls," she said as she handed Mackenzie a few Free Drink vouchers and made her exit, leaving the four of us to ponder our next move.

Inside the main bar area, a DJ worked the dense crowd into a frenzy, the laser lights flashing in perfect harmony with the music. Darcy pointed to a booth near the side edge of the dance floor and didn't wait another second. She zoomed through the crowd to claim it for us. Mackenzie grabbed me by the hand and dragged me over.

The last thing I wanted was to raise suspicions, and there I was, already struggling to keep my distractions down to a minimum. The thing was, I needed to find Heather Martin if I was going to help her beat the demon destroying her life. Without her, this plan wasn't going to go anywhere.

We started with a round of drinks first, with Darcy and me heading to the bar while the other two held the booth.

I ordered a drink called a Ginger Snap and a lemon soda for Mackenzie, who insisted on not drinking on account of her driving. Darcy got a Mojito and brought back a Cosmo for

Brianna. It was really awesome knowing they were completely free.

Despite the crowd and the music feeling almost suffocating, I kept my peripheral awareness turned to the maximum as I searched for any hint of either Heather, Kane, or the faces I remembered from the previous time I'd seen them. During the walk back to our booth, I scanned a lot of the other booths but didn't see anybody of interest.

We ended up heading out to the dance floor after that first drink, and just like the last time I was there, it wasn't long before the rhythm of the music consumed me, pulling me into its addictive grip with little resistance. I closed my eyes, feeling my friends around me as I let myself go and moved in time with the beat.

One song rolled into the next with little transition, the thumping bass dragging each melody through to the next. I got completely immersed in those sounds. The light drinks were just enough to numb the edges of my nerves. About an hour in, Brianna tapped Darcy on the shoulder to say that she needed to go to the bathroom, and Mackenzie decided to go with them. I watched them work through the crowd toward their destination. And that's when it happened, the adrenalin hitting my system like a freight train.

Sitting in a booth up on the second level, I saw the man I came to end. He sat closest to the railing amongst half a dozen or so friends. I walked up some stairs to get a visual of all the girls sitting at the adjoining booth. I saw Heather seated between two other girls, one of whom I recognized as the one I questioned during my previous visit. The mood amongst the girls didn't appear to be anywhere near the level of the boys, who I could see appearing to be taking turns snorting something off a small plate, and they kept passing between each other.

Staring at the two booths robbed me of my dancing moves in a heartbeat, and after telling Darcy I needed to sit down, she waved me away as she continued dancing with some guy who appeared to have taken an interest. Her new friend offered me a weak smile when he saw me check him out, and I returned it before turning back to our own table.

A waitress came and took a drink order for me, and I decided to go for a soda to keep my senses alert. Despite telling my friends so, drinking and dancing wasn't what I had come for, and I needed to go to work if I was going to get through the minefield of obstacles sitting between me and success.

I could barely see both Kane's and Heather's booths from my own, and while sipping a drink, I watched half the girls make their way down to the dance floor and claim their spot almost directly below the boys. Kane took a couple of looks over the railing while continuing to drink and snort whatever drugs they had going on between them. He didn't appear as aggressive as I'd seen him in the past, but I knew guys like him could turn in a heartbeat.

With my own booth slightly elevated, I could see most of the dance floor and found Mackenzie and Brianna back dancing near Darcy, who appeared to have begun getting close to her new friend, close enough for them to start embracing each other. The other two watched on and shook their heads, but their grins showed no malice intent behind them. I was happy for Darcy. She'd had a rough trot herself with boyfriends, and I knew she craved some male attention, having been single for almost a year.

Leaving Darcy alone in the middle of the dance floor with her new man, the other two came back to the booth for some rest and a drink. Rather than summon the waitress, Mackenzie instead went up to the bar, while Brianna stayed with me while she checked her phone. That was when I happened to glance back up to the second level and saw Kane reach across the table and grab one of the guys by the shirt. He pulled him close as he leaned in and appeared to hiss something into his face. The others froze as they watched on, and while I couldn't hear what was being said. It was apparent there had been some sort of disagreement.

"There you are," I whispered to myself as I watched the real Kane Nazif emerge, the one I knew existed behind that fake facade he so easily put up at will. He let go of the guy and waved for him to go away, almost as if he owned the table they sat at. At first, the guy didn't move, but when a couple of the others also began to gesture for him to get up, he finally stood up and left the group. Feeling triumphant, Kane leaned back in his seat, shaking his head as he looked down at his girl, and that's when I saw a smile slowly birth across his face, a smile that screamed pure contempt.

Call it intuition or fate or whatever you want, but seeing that face was what prompted me to prepare the syringe. I didn't want to put the inevitable off any longer and also didn't want to risk missing an opportunity if it presented itself. I'd watched plenty of crime movies on TV to know the basics.

"Heading to the bathroom," I told Brianna, grabbed my purse, and off I went. Just as it had been the last time I was there, the toilets again overflowed with people surrounding the sinks in front of the mirrors.

I stopped in front of the mirror and looked at my reflection. It wasn't my hair or makeup or the cleanliness of my dress I was checking on. What I was staring at was the person hidden behind the eyes, the avenging angel concealed behind the face of a regular nurse helping to save the lives of vulnerable women. I almost felt a warmth of courage fire up inside me, as if a sign from the soul within.

After a deep breath, I headed for the door and passed by the bar. In the distance, I could see dozens of people continuing to dance their way through the latest tunes. I often found myself escaping reality through music. I paused when I reached the archway and scanned the dance floor. I quickly saw Heather Martin still dancing amongst her friends. Sitting at our booth were Darcy and Brianna, her phone still firmly in hand.

I was about to head back to our table to mentally prepare myself for the next step when someone suddenly pushed past me hard enough to send me stumbling forward. I managed to grab someone's arm to stop myself from falling over, apologized, and looked behind me to see Kane walk past. That was the first time our eyes met, and with an indifferent look of that same arrogance, I knew there wouldn't be an apology coming from him. He barely noticed, the conceit carrying him to where Heather continued dancing.

Feeling a lot more than nerves gripping my insides, I wanted to scream at him, to run up and stab that syringe directly into his eyeball. I visualized doing so, and the vision of him screaming while cupping the wound only served to further fuel the anger driving me. He took a few steps on the dance floor, propelled through the crowd, and grabbed Heather's arm. Caught unaware, she tried to pull back before realizing who it was, and Kane pulled her toward him as I saw the pain on her face.

Leaning close to her, Kane yelled something she didn't like into her ear, and I watched as Heather shook her head, almost pleading with him to let her go. I couldn't decipher what he was instructing her to do, but I knew that if it was to leave the club, then I was out of time. I slung the purse over my shoulder and held the syringe low in front of me as I walked toward them. When I got closer, I removed the cap off the needle, carefully navigating my way through the crowd as I kept my eyes on Kane and Heather. The music never hesitates, while the club lights flash in vibrant hues, creating an electric atmosphere on the dance floor.

I was a few feet from Kane; my right arm was hanging down in front of me, using my left to fend off anybody dancing their way into me. I could hear Kane shouting at Heather, who continued trying to change his mind about whatever he wanted from her. I passed the last person standing between us and braced myself. My hand firmly held the needle, with my thumb pressed ever so slightly on the plunger.

I barely slowed as I passed by. In the blink of an eye, I swung my hand like a pendulum, the syringe arcing down to the floor and then up again before embedding itself into the underside of his left butt cheek. I used all of my medical training to make sure I timed the delivery perfectly, the needle in and out with just a split second in between to deliver the narcotic.

It took just a few feet for the crowd to swallow me up again, ditching the needle in my purse. Only when I reached the other side of the dance floor did I dare to stop and look behind me. Kane still had a hold of Heather's arm while talking into her ear, but I could see his other hand rubbing the spot where I injected him. All I could do then was sit back and wait.

"Hey, Liz, meet Harry," Darcy called out to me when I got back to the booth. She pointed to the same guy she'd been smooching with.

"Hey," I said, gave his outstretched hand a shake, and then I sat down.

"Harry's a cop from Charleston," Darcy continued when he took the seat next to her.

"You're a long way from home," I said, looking behind them as I saw Kane finally drag Heather from the dance floor. Surprisingly, they didn't head to the exit but instead reappeared sitting at their respective booths a few minutes later. It appeared as if he didn't like his girl to be out of his reach.

Despite both Darcy and Harry trying to have a conversation with me, I had very good reason for struggling to keep my concentration on them. What I wanted was to focus on Kane, visualizing the drug slowly working its way through the fat and muscle of his buttock and leaking into his bloodstream. Time was all that stood between him and whatever reaction his body would have to the drug inside him.

Sitting there waiting for something to happen felt like the longest surprise of my life. Minutes felt like hours as I continued listening to Harry telling me about one of his friends who was arriving in town the following day before Darcy joined in, trying to arrange some sort of double date. The only reason I agreed was because I wanted to shut them up so I could focus on Kane.

Forty minutes. That's how long it took for me to notice the first sign that something wasn't quite right with Kane, and even then, I wasn't sure it was because of anything I'd done to him. Kane's aggression returned, and while Darcy and Harry continued the smooching they'd now resumed in the booth, I watched him reach across the table and again grab one of his companions by the shirt.

This time, the outcome wasn't exactly the same as the previous time, with his friend not exactly willing to put up with being manhandled. He shrugged Kane's hand off before slapping it away. This only led Kane to half-stand before trying to grab his friend's shirt a second time with both hands. When the friend again deflected his hands away, Kane ramped things up considerably. He lunged across the table with one arm swinging, the fist connected flush on the face where blood immediately flowed from the friend's nose. Others stood and tried pulling the two men apart. It was the first time I heard Kane's familiar voice as he screamed over the music.

I couldn't quite make out what he yelled, but the volume alone brought the attention of a lot of people to their part of the club. Even Darcy and Harry paused to look up to the second level.

"Looks like someone's had enough to drink," Harry said before gently pulling Darcy's face back around with a finger on the side of her chin.

"Quite," she managed to say before locking her lips onto his.

Brianne barely looked up from her phone, utterly disinterested in the exchange. I did spot Mackenzie dancing with another group of girls near the outer edge of the dance floor, and considering her proximity to some of the speakers, I could see she wasn't in a position to hear anything other than music.

Up on the second level, the guy with the bleeding nose left the area and walked down to the dance floor, where Heather once again left the second floor to go dancing with his girlfriend. He walked up to them, and I watched the girl immediately try to help him as she panicked at the sight of her man's blood dripping from his nose. The group made their way to the outer edge of the dance area, and kind of leaned against a table as the girl tried cleaning her boyfriend's face with some napkins.

Looking back up to the second level, I could see Kane pacing, his hands grasping the top of his head as he continued yelling something at nobody in particular. I wasn't sure whether he was trying to keep his anger under control or just trying to make a spectacle of himself, the volume of his voice loud enough for me to just make out the words.

"He better not," he screamed. "I'm telling you he...," but that was when someone tried to pull him down into one of the booths.

"Can I get past, please? I'll be back," Brianna suddenly said from beside me, and I stood to let her out. I watched her walk toward Mackenzie for a few seconds before turning my attention back up to the second level, but Kane was gone. So had the rest of his party.

I'm not sure whether it was panic or just curiosity, but I desperately tried to find Kane again. I knew he wouldn't just leave, not when Heather remained on the dance floor. It was while watching her that I spotted Kane walking through the crowd toward the group. The girl cleaning her boyfriend's face had her back turned from everyone else, which was why she didn't see Kane approaching and couldn't brace herself for what happened next.

Time seemed to slow as a multitude of scenarios suddenly took hold of me. I watched Kane first shove the girl violently aside before he reached out and grabbed the bleeding guy by the scruff of the shirt with both hands. The girl yelled out in shock as she hit the ground hard, sending a group of dancers scattering as others knelt down to help her. My guess is they assumed she'd simply tripped and weren't aware of the explosive situation about to unfold.

"I TOLD YOU TO LEAVE MY GIRL ALONE," was what Kane yelled out, and he launched two punches in rapid succession. It was also at that very moment I remembered one distinct side effect an overdose could cause...intense paranoia.

"I HAVEN'T TOUCHED YOUR GIRL," the other guy yelled back as he tried to dodge the punches with little effect. His nose took a punch square on but managed to dodge the rest of the headshots.

"I KNOW YOU DID," Kane screamed, thrust a knee up into the guy's groin, and pushed him back into the wall. The girl who'd taken a tumble suddenly jumped onto Kane's back and wrapped her arms around his neck as Heather began screaming for Kane to stop.

That was when security finally arrived, and that should have been the end of it. I considered my attempt a complete failure by this point and would have gladly left things alone for another day, when things took a sudden turn. One security guard held the girl and managed to pull her arms free, while a second guard tried to grab Kane by the wrist. He might have succeeded were it not for Heather suddenly stumbling between them and tripping over someone when Kane slapped her face away.

Again, I watched Kane run his fingers across the top of his head as if trying to clutch his thoughts together. The fingers grabbed hold of his hair, squeezed, and pulled in separate directions as he grimaced in pain, frustration, or whatever sensation had hold of him.

"SCREW YOU, KANE," the bleeding guy suddenly shouted out, and that was when Kane reached behind his back and pulled out a gun. He swung it around in a wide arc before aiming the barrel directly into the unfortunate friend's face.

By this stage, the entire club had stopped to watch the spectacle unfold, nobody expecting it to end the way it did. What I hadn't noticed was Harry leaving Darcy's side to go and help the security guys get Kane under control. It wasn't until Darcy screamed at the sight of the gun, which was when I looked at her. By the time I focused on what was happening in front of her, it was Harry with his own weapon drawn and shouted, "POLICE, DROP YOUR WEAPON."

In my mind, I pictured Kane realizing he stood no chance and throwing his gun on the floor in front of him. The security guys would jump him, force him to the floor, and contain him before calling law enforcement. That's what I was expecting to see, but that wasn't what happened. Instead, Kane grabbed his head with his left hand, and the other holding the pistol pressed to the side of his face as he appeared in misery. Others watching must have assumed him crazy and trying to control whatever demons he had in his head, but I knew better. It was a massive dose coursing through his system, mixing with whatever else he'd been snorting earlier and turning his brain into a fried tangle of mush.

I think I saw the moment he decided that his only option was to fight, that final flash of arrogance finally betraying him for the last time. He opened his eyes and stared at Harry. Henry repeated to him to drop his weapon. In the blink of an eye, Kane's face morphed from confusion to conviction as he stared down the new threat, standing just a few feet away. He never made it. Harry barely managed to utter Stop a final time before he fired twice, both bullets hitting Kane in the middle of his chest.

Screams erupted from every corner of the club as complete chaos ensued. The majority of people simply fell to the floor while a few made a break for the doors, which ultimately led to a stampede of everybody else standing. My attention remained on Kane, who fell back against the table behind him while clutching his chest. That's where I expected the story to end for him, but with an extra fuel source running through his system, I don't think he was quite ready to give up.

"DROP YOUR WEAPON," Harry screamed as people continued running past the scene.

Kane's white t-shirt quickly turned into a horror scene as the blood from the two bullet holes began to change the color of his outfit. I noticed Heather standing a few feet behind Harry for safety, frozen to the spot as she watched her boyfriend desperately sucking air into his punctured lungs. In the moments before the final exchange, I think it was Heather that Kane saw standing behind the cop, and I think he planned to take her with him.

He zeroed in on her as he began to raise the hand holding the gun but never got close to lining her up enough to take the shot. Harry fired a third and final shot into his chest; the gun's explosion caused those watching to flinch one final time before Kane fell forward onto his face. Harry stepped forward, and kicked the gun from his hand, and that's when the reign of Kane Nazif came to an end.

Chapter 16

The rest of that morning went by like a movie reel, one that started and stopped with brief flashes of monologue as if offering nothing more than highlights. First, the sheriff's deputies arrived and secured the scene before taking note of any witnesses who remained. Both Mackenzie and Darcy insisted on waiting behind to make sure that Ellie was OK, as she wasn't handling the horrific events very well. That ended up putting the four of us on the list of witnesses, and there was a possibility of being called in for an interview if one was deemed necessary.

After an initial check of the scene, a couple of deputies took Harry downtown, and once Ellie assured us she was alright, Darcy caught an Uber down to the sheriff's department. The rest of us drove home in relative silence and dropped Brianna off first before Mackenzie took me home.

By the time I walked into my apartment, my stomach felt like I'd swallowed something that I never ate. The feeling alone was enough to send me running for the toilet. I couldn't help but remember the way I had felt after the whole Brian Hurst thing.

This time, however, there was no confusion. Kane Nazif was surely and truly dead, the man gunned down in front of dozens of witnesses. His blood had decorated more than just the front of his shirt. The horrific scene permanently burnt into the minds of all those who witnessed the shooting. The image that kept returning to me wasn't the final shot that killed him, but the way he kept clutching at his head, unsure of why he was feeling the way he did. It was that very confusion that his paranoia elevated to such an extent that he found it impossible to handle.

I was tired, yes, but not entirely sure I'd be able to sleep. For the first hour, I sat alone out on the balcony, watching the sky grow ever lighter with the arrival of a new day. The shadows of night began to slowly fade as a bluish tinge emerged over the far horizon. I could see the first signs of it between a couple of trees, one advantage of being up on the second floor as I gazed across the roofs of nearby homes.

A Trinity knot cross necklace that I'd inherited from my grandmother upon her death was what I liked to hold whenever confronted with uncertainty. I'd begun wearing it the day of her funeral and hadn't taken it off since. I think, in a way, it became a sort of safety blanket for me. Feeling it between my fingers somehow gave me a sense of protection, as if my grandmother herself was sitting right there beside me.

I think what I was grappling with wasn't the act of killing these men, or at least playing a part in their deaths. In my eyes, and I guess in the eyes of fate itself, they had earned their early retirement thanks to the many years of abuse they had dealt out to those unfortunate enough to have been caught within their grasp. No, what I think I grappled with was the finality of death itself, the realization that there was no coming back. What if I made a mistake?

When the leading edge of the sun finally broke across that horizon, and the first rays caused me to squint my eyes, I found an unwavering urge to sleep. My head felt heavy, the night needing to come to an end before I allowed my imagination to run away completely. No amount of thinking was going to change the past, and I needed to move on and turn my attention to the future.

I headed back inside and checked the front door to make sure it was locked. Along the way to my room, I picked up my cell phone and turned it to silent after making sure no random alarm was set for later that afternoon. I hated it when that happened, especially during a much-needed sleep.

Not only did I end up sleeping for nine uninterrupted hours, but I woke up feeling a lot better about things than I did when I laid down. It actually felt as if some otherworldly being came down and rearranged my thoughts in such a way as to logically clarify everything that had happened. Destiny was the one who had arranged for me to meet each of the men I'd helped end, and it was destiny who I would continue to work with.

Destiny wasn't the only one who came calling during my sleep. Peg also sent me a message asking if I was awake and could let her in. It appeared as if she'd dropped by my place just after two, but with me in deep sleep, I didn't hear her knocking at all. I sent her a reply before climbing out of bed, and then she called my phone.

"Hey," I said after swiping the call to life.

"Oh my God, are you alright? Ellie told me what happened."

"Yeah, I'm fine. How is she, though? She looked a mess when we left. Kind of felt bad leaving her."

"No, she's good, honest," Peg said as I sat on the couch and pulled my legs in close to my chest. "Her business partner took over and has been dealing with the fallout."

"That was one crazy night," I said, feeling a tinge of guilt for not being honest. "Talk about insane."

"Apparently, he'd taken a heap of drugs during the night and lashed out at a couple of his friends."

"Really?"

"Yeah, Darcy told me that the cop she was with, told her, that it looked like he might have been on a really bad trip."

"You mean Darcy's new man?"

"New man?"

"Oh, she hasn't told you?" I could hear the teenaged anticipation in Peg's voice, something girls never really grew out of.

"No, but please do."

Graphic incident aside, I filled Peg in on the details of Darcy's apparent new boyfriend, a cop who lived on the other side of town. In fact, I even saw some intimacy between the two, which made me think that their running into each other at the club was no coincidence. Peg lapped it up, of course, every single word, some juicy bit of gossip that would satisfy her need until the next one. It was a trait many might have frowned on, but Peg wasn't the kind to spread it, especially if untrue. She just enjoyed hearing things like an avid daytime soapy fan.

We must have spent almost an hour chatting before she had to go, and I promised to catch up with her during my next shift. When I ended the call, I turned my attention to some of the news sites to try and read anything about the JJ's shooting, but there wasn't much to find. Only one site mentioned that someone threatened patrons with a gun before being shot by an off-duty policeman, and that was it.

I wasn't sure what I had been expecting to find, but the brief story was almost disappointing because of the lack of details. It actually felt more like filler, some random event thrown in to bulk up what looked like a slow-news kind of day. What made me smile was the vision of Kane Nazif looking up from wherever he sat in hell, screaming about the lack of attention his death had garnered. He probably envisioned much more climactic fanfare for his eventual departure from this world.

"I bet you didn't see that coming," I mumbled under my breath as I set the phone down on the coffee table and headed to the kitchen for some food.

The one thought that kept returning to me when I watched my scrambled eggs cooking a few minutes later was how each death I'd been involved in just happened to appear self-inflicted. I'm not sure whether I was being naive or even delusional, but I believed that there was definitely something working with me to make all of these incidents play out in just the right way to avoid indicting me in the deaths. What I didn't want was for me to grow more confident than I should, believing that I was somehow above the possibility of getting caught and making some dumb mistake that would lead to my downfall.

It was that very possibility that ended up haunting me for the next couple of days, days I spent distracting myself with movies and books and all the unhealthy snacks I could consume. No matter how hard I tried to turn my attention elsewhere, it wasn't enough to keep the same questioning thoughts from slowly returning, my brain constantly see-sawing from one extreme to the other. It was only when I went back to the hospital on Monday night that I finally managed to find the one activity that actually helped distract me...work.

It was during that first shift back after the whole Kane situation, that I finally found something in a newspaper that somebody had left in the lunchroom. It was the first break I'd been able to take after six straight hours, and I took full advantage. An article three paragraphs made mention of a bad batch of cocaine working its way through the community, leading to a number of violent incidents, including a couple of shootings, with one at a grocery store and another at a nightclub. No mention was made about one of the shooters having been unknowingly injected with an extra dose shortly before he began his paranoid attack.

I must have read the article at least three times before Peg's voice suddenly pulled my attention away from the newspaper.

"Eliza, someone for you in Room 8," she said from behind me and disappeared again before I could ask for clarification. Who would ask for me? In all the years I'd spent working at the hospital, I had never had someone come in asking for me specifically. Adrenalin hit my system while I rinsed my cup out and walked out of the lunchroom, and a shocking thought suddenly hit me. What if the police had finally made some connection, and this was a detective coming to take me in?

Why would they come in the middle of the night? The logical side of my brain came back nearly immediately, and it was right, of course. Why would they?

Unable to shake the feeling that my luck had finally run out, I felt my knees weaken with each step as I walked down that corridor, completely oblivious to the rest of the commotion in our facility. In the distance, I saw the sign for Room 8 sticking out from the end of the dividing wall as if taunting me. Just before reaching for the door, I stopped and took a couple of deep breaths, certain that I would find more than just one person waiting for me, an entire squad ready to take a suspected serial killer into custody.

My trembling fingers could barely hang on to the door as I slightly opened and forced a smile. The man sitting in the chair flinched a little, my arrival catching him off-guard.

"I'm sorry for keeping you waiting," I said as I pushed the door wide open. I couldn't place the man's face. It took me a second or two, but not recognizing him was just another confirmation that a stranger asking for me specifically meant that it had to be some sort of law enforcement officer.

"Oh, no big deal," the man said and offered me a warm smile, one that looked surprisingly genuine.

"I'm Nurse Moore, you asked for me?" That was when he threw me a bit of a curveball, one that took me a moment to fully comprehend.

"Actually, I don't mind who fixes my little mishap," was what he said as he held up a loosely bandaged hand.

"I'm sorry?" Seeing the bandage threw me off, as did his rugged good looks. He had the kind of smile that held an air of mystery about it, a chiseled chin defining the rest of his features.

"My cut? I just came here to get it looked at."

That was when I realized the error of my ways; the assumption that someone had asked for me specifically caused me to be totally off the mark.

"I'm so sorry," I said as I felt heat in my cheeks, sure that fierce coloring would quickly follow. He was a patient, a genuinely injured patient needing treatment, and not some law enforcement officer coming to arrest me.

"That's quite alright," the man said. "I wasn't trying to be difficult."

"No, no, not at all," I said as I went to work, first inspecting the cut and then cleaning it in preparation for the doctor who'd examine the patient for any needed stitches or necessary medication.

While I was working on him, he introduced himself as Don Marlow, a crypto trader who had just purchased himself a new Groodle puppy named Biscuit. It was the pup who ultimately caused his injury when he tried quietening her crying with some canned food and subsequently sliced his thumb during the process of opening the can.

"Guess I shouldn't be opening anything when I was still half asleep," he joked. When I finished cleaning his cut, I guessed he would need at least two stitches, if not three.

"Probably best to wait until you're wide awake," I offered.

"Say, that necklace you're wearing. That's Celtic, is it not?"

"Yes, it is," I said, quite surprised by his observation. "Very good."

"No, I'm sorry, I wasn't trying to impress you. It's just that my grandmother used to wear a similar one, except hers was made from rose gold." I was about to ask him about it, but that was when Dr. Bryce walked in and took over.

Twenty minutes later, Don Marlow was the proud owner of three new stitches in his left thumb. He thanked the doctor for helping him out. While I tidied up and Dr. Bryce left, Don leaned in a little closer to keep his shy request between us.

"I'm not usually prone to asking random nurses out for coffee this early in the morning, but maybe today just feels like it's worth taking a chance?"

"Coffee?"

"Yes, I assume you drink it since you work the night shift?"

"Yes, of course," I said, again feeling silly with my near-childish shyness.

I usually don't let someone's good looks bother me, but this time, I couldn't shake the feeling.

"Coffee would be great. I finish at six if that's alright with you."

He grinned as I felt more heat fill my cheeks.

"Six is perfect. How about the Starbucks a couple of blocks down?"

"I'll meet you there?"

"Done deal," he said and actually held his good hand out to shake mine.

When I walked into work the previous evening, I did so with the assumption that I could use the shift as a distraction from everything that had happened. The last thing I expected was to find myself agreeing to a coffee date with someone I didn't know a thing about. And maybe I'll get to know him better if the situation allows it.

Chapter 17

The date with Don Marlow, if you could call it that, went as well as expected, given that I had no preconceived ideas about it. The man had appeared completely out of the blue. In terms of romantic interest, even after sharing a coffee with him, I still wasn't entirely sure I wanted to pursue the idea of a relationship. It wasn't that I didn't find him both physically and intellectually attractive...on the contrary. In fact, I saw him charming in all sorts of mannerisms, and I definitely enjoyed being in his presence. But the problem is that I've been having inevitable distractions lately, and I wasn't sure it would mix with a new romance.

We sat chatting for almost an hour before a couple of successive yawns from me brought the morning to an end. When I first yawned, he asked whether he was keeping me awake or putting me to sleep, and once a second one came almost immediately after, he broke into laughter, and color filled my cheeks for the third time that morning.

While we didn't make specific plans for another date, we did exchange phone numbers, and I have to admit, I felt reassured as I got into my Civic and observed him walking toward his Silverado. At 6'3", he had just the right height to easily slide in behind the wheel without having to step up into the cabin of his truck. When he rolled past me a few seconds later, he gave me a wave before accelerating off into morning traffic.

Despite being tired and yawning twice before starting my engine, I didn't want to go home. I wasn't ready to call an end to the day just yet, not when my brain felt baffled. I needed to try and find some clarity, and for me, there was only one place I ever seemed to find it, and that was sitting with my grandmother.

The day wasn't exactly starting out with glorious sunshine, a thick band of clouds hanging heavy above the city blocking most of the rays. I didn't think it would rain, but I decided I wasn't going to let that stop me from trying to find some clarity the way I usually did when visiting the cemetery.

Given the early hour, there weren't nearly as many people, just a couple of cars in the cemetery's parking lot. I parked closer to the far left, given the proximity to my Grandma's gravesite, and climbed out as a southern breeze began blowing through the nearby trees. The sound of the leaves rustling instantly set the tone, and I already knew I had come to the right place.

Before sitting down in front of the grave, I first swept a few wayward leaves from the top of the headstone. Finally, I gave the top of the marker a kiss, walked back to the end of the grave, and sat down. At first, I heard the low rumble of distant traffic, the breeze through the trees not quite loud enough to come out on top, but when the wind changed directions, the sound of traffic all but disappeared. Even the clouds seemed to want to help out, the thick blanket parting a few moments after I sat and giving the sun's rays just enough space to light up the place.

Five minutes turned into ten, and ten into twenty, as I found myself sitting in complete silence and enjoying the peace and tranquility of the place. At one point, I leaned back on the grass and closed my eyes, feeling the warmth of the sunshine on my face. I could have easily fallen asleep, and maybe I did for a few minutes, but the thoughts swirling around in the back of my mind were never far away.

I whispered some words barely loud enough for me to hear.

"Grandma, do you think God could ever forgive me for what I've done?"

I wasn't too spiritual as I had to work most of my weekends, but I know plenty of my friends and colleagues were. Grandma always said everything comes down to a personal choice, and you're either living for God or against Him. It seemed that killing abusive men could have disrupted that line of thinking. Which was probably why I asked the question that I did. Would God understand the reasons for my actions and actually forgive me?

Instead of waiting for an answer that most likely wouldn't come knocking on my door right then and there, I began to share the details of what had happened at the club with my grandma. Each time I spoke, I took a quick look around to make sure we were alone, and nobody had snuck up to one of the adjoining graves. I should point out that in the years since I'd been coming to the cemetery, I'd only ever seen one person a single time attend any of the four plots on either side. Their poor condition is a surefire sign that they didn't get too many visitors throughout the year.

I believe the hardest part for me at that moment was realizing that there was no turning back from what was already done. That and the constant wondering of whether I was overreacting to the brutality. My involvement in three deaths already put me into the serial killer category, and yet I felt no such affiliation to such a title. How would the rest of the world view me if they knew the truth?

"Am I doing the right thing, Grandma?"

That was the real question I needed to find an answer to, perhaps the only question worth asking. Feeling a lot like a lost child in the woods, I wasn't sure whether that one or any of the other questions or insecurities would ever find answers, but that was when a scream suddenly rose into the air from somewhere nearby. I rose up onto my knees and scanned around the immediate area but couldn't see anything. When I pushed myself up onto my feet, that was when I saw a man and a woman in a physical altercation several rows over from me.

From where I stood, it didn't look like a mugging or anything that intense, but rather a husband and wife fighting over something small that the man kept trying to hold out of reach. The woman kept trying to jump and snatch the object, which the man repeatedly waved in front of her face before pulling it away again. Car keys? When the woman managed to grab hold of the keyring, the man smacked her hand away and took a step back before again dangling it in front of her face.

"Hey," I called out.

When neither of them appeared to hear me, I walked between the headstones and called out a second time.

"HEY!"

This time, they not only heard me, but the man handed the keys over before sending me a wave and a muffled apology I could barely make out. The woman grabbed the keys, bent down, picked up her purse, and then walked toward the cemetery's main exit, where she took a look over her shoulder at the man still standing there. He suddenly looked over to her as if summoned and reluctantly walked toward her.

I watched the couple until they climbed into the same car and drove away before returning to my grandmother's grave. Only when I sat down a second time did I possibly see a puzzling exchange as the answer I'd been hoping for? Call it a stretch, but given the way they abruptly stopped when I interrupted their argument, it made it feel as if my intervention had prevented the fight from escalating. Wasn't that precisely what I had been doing with the three couples from my recent past?

Throughout the Bible, there have been a few times when God allowed enemies to conquer His people. I remember Grandma telling me that Egypt enslaved the Israelites for 400 years. The Philistines defeated the Israelites and took the Arc of Covenants. Babylon and Assyria conquered His people and led them to exile. And she showed me in Jeremiah, where God issued Israel a certificate of divorce because of their continued unfaithfulness. Even when Jesus preached the Gospel, the Jews rejected Him and had Him killed... The world is full of bad people!

Goosebumps broke out across my skin as I had an overwhelming sense of approval filling my very soul. I don't actually know whether it was approval or a personal acknowledgment, but whatever it was, it gave me the answer I'd been looking for.

When I left the cemetery that morning, I felt as if I'd been handed the keys to fate itself, a kind of free pass to deal out justice to the world's abusers. Some might have seen it as my ego growing too big too fast, but that's not how I saw it. Those first three killings felt like a kind of traineeship, destiny or fate or whatever you want to call it, testing me to see whether I could handle the pressure of terminating these terrible people. Maybe it was to see whether I'd take things too far, maybe unleash the kind of brutality their abuse warranted.

When I showed that I could intervene in ways that didn't require gratuitous amounts of violence, maybe that was when the powers that be decided I was the right person for the job. Perhaps I'd passed the traineeship and was now qualified for the role.

"Just give me some business cards," I whispered to myself when I climbed back into the Civic, feeling a new sense of purpose as I rejoined the morning's traffic and headed home.

Chapter 18

The days turned into weeks, and in a way, life returned to the same mundane existence I'd lived before the first killing. I spent some spare time searching for any hint of domestic violence. Still, for some reason, there just wasn't anything coming through the hospital channels. On one side of the coin, that's really super awesome because nobody likes living through that nonsense.

On the other side, we received reports through our e-mail stating over 50,000 men and women are killed globally every year. Interestingly, 80% of the totals were from men. Which is equivalent to 136 lives per day. Some of these reports really make you think.

Whenever I scanned the news sites or social media, the only cases I would find were ones where the victims had already fallen to their abusers. I read this case about a lady named Jennifer who convinced her boyfriend to shoot her husband. I was really taken back by all these women who use GoFundMe accounts to accomplish so many harmful acts.

It's another terrible situation when we see some lady with three to five children from different fathers while she's collecting child support from each one. Talk about a different type of victim that claims the heart of a dollar. I know not all men are evil. The abuse associated with women seems to be psychological or manipulative in nature, while men are more commonly recognized for their physical aggression or temper issues.

At one point, I was researching how three single mothers were killed by boyfriends within the span of just ten days. A married mother of four also died the following week. Her estranged husband broke into their house and murdered the woman right after their children had left for school.

I felt incredibly frustrated reading those stories, and it filled me with such a sense of urgency that I found myself scouring every possible platform for abused victims for an hour each day. Urgency might be too loose of a term, but how else can I describe the feeling of reading about the deaths of men or women whom I had the power to end?

Knowing there were people out there who needed to be stopped before things got out of control is something beyond simple frustration. I began to expand my searches to places outside of my immediate vicinity in the hope that I wouldn't waste any more time waiting for a case to fall into my lap. And that's when it happened; just three days after spreading the parameters of my search out past a hundred miles from Odessa, I came across a video of a young woman crying inconsolably while pleading for help into the camera, her face almost beaten to a pulp.

That was the first time I laid eyes on Renee Ross, a young nineteen-year-old girl who lived in the small town of Slaton, which itself sat just outside of Lubbock. That put her about 130 miles north of Odessa and not exactly close enough for me to deal with while maintaining my own life.

It wasn't easy finding her, that's for sure, but it's amazing what can be achieved through the power of VPNs, fake social media profiles, and a bit of detective work using other people's posts. The first thing I did after coming across the video was to bookmark it to the fake profile, a great layer of incognito protection on popular platforms. I figured that it would be a waste of time going to the trouble of using a brand new laptop and cell phone if I would then just sign in with my personal accounts.

So many people responded to that initial video that girl posted. Multiple offers were made to help her out with temporary accommodations. From what I could find, it looked like she accepted one specific woman's offer of help, which was a good thing. But it wasn't mainly her welfare that I was interested in. As far as I was concerned, my focus was on the boyfriend, the one responsible for causing those injuries in the first place, and boy, did I open Pandora's Box once I found him.

Douglas Randall was what you might call a daddy's boy. This twenty-two-year-old high school dropout who leeched off his wealthy and disinterested father as much as possible. Doug Senior spent most of his time out of town on business trips, a corporate jet setter. One might say he was representing his company's interest in farming equipment that he sold to large conglomerates all around the world. While Doug leaned into the comforts of his father's fortune, he filled his days with aimless pursuits and an ever-growing sense of entitlement, oblivious to the reality of the struggles faced by those outside his sheltered life.

And what did Doug Junior get up to while Daddy was out of town? Absolutely nothing when it came to some kind of career. Instead, I followed a trail of destruction involving more than a dozen girlfriends, several abortions, and surprisingly, a taste for bullying small business owners into a protection racket operated by himself and almost a dozen friends. As I said, it's incredible how much a person can find using social media and city records.

I turned my attention to the girlfriends first, and what I found just about sent me into a rage. All but two had multiple posts going back almost six years with stories of abuse, most only speaking up after managing to break free. Out of all the men I had come in contact with during my newfound job, Douglas Randall was by far the worst, a serial abuser who would never change, not given his protective father who preferred to pay anytime his son needed to beat some sort of charge. It's a wonder nobody else had already stepped in and ended him.

After studying Randall for more than a week, I ended up finding myself caught in somewhat of a situation. While he did fit the profile of someone I needed to meet perfectly, the issue I had was the distance between us, a spread that wasn't exactly a cakewalk. We're talking at least a four-hour round trip, no easy task when trying to remain under the radar. My life wouldn't just take a back seat while I spent endless driving back and forth in the hopes of coming across some ingenuous way of ending him on the spur of the moment.

I found myself more and more distracted while working the night shift. When Don Marlow began to show even more interest in me, it began to interfere with the only time I had to pursue the abuser. It didn't feel like the smooth operation I had been used to. As far as I could tell, given the lack of any follow-up from law enforcement, the first three went off without a hitch. So why was this one, the one I considered the worst of them all, so tough to get to?

If Donnie hadn't been so charming, I think I would have cut him off the second I realized his presence was interfering with my work, but the truth was, I liked him...like, really liked him. He was smart, and funny, and he knew things that ordinary people didn't know, like stuff about history, science, and space, and just anything and everything. I could listen to him talk for hours while sipping wine under the stars. He just felt so...warm.

It was during one of our dates that the answer finally came to me, an answer to a question I had been asking myself for almost ten days.

"I have to fly to Reno on Tuesday," was what he told me as we sat on his couch watching a ballgame. "There's a conference happening that I really need to attend."

"How long for?"

"A week, I'd say. I have a brother who lives near Fernley, and he's asked me to drop in for a few days."

"Oh, OK," I said.

"You sound disappointed," he said, surprising me. "You want to come?"

"No, I can't. I have work," I said, but the truth was, the second I heard his plans, my brain began to form one of my own, a plan I had been painstakingly trying to find for too long.

"That sucks. You would enjoy my brother's ranch."

"Really? Maybe another time?"

"For sure," he said, noticed my empty beer, and offered me a fresh one.

That was when a thought came to me, one that I hadn't even come close to considering before. I could take my own vacation, pretend to be going somewhere else, but instead head to Lubbock to find and take care of Douglas Junior. The idea must have hit me quite hard because it wasn't long before Donnie asked whether I was OK with him going, noting my sudden distraction.

"Yes, honestly, I'm fine," I told him at one point, annunciating the fine to make sure he understood, but he did look at me with a funny expression. It looked almost cute, him thinking that his intended absence was what bothered me. If he only knew the truth.

We still hadn't gotten to that part of our relationship, if you know what I mean. Donnie dropped me back home around midnight because nothing good happens after midnight. A kiss was how we said goodnight and not just a random peck. To say I was keen on him was an understatement, and I could see in the way he looked at me that he felt the same. It was because of my alter-ego activities that I couldn't entirely give in to those feelings, although I didn't dare to push anything either. Once we separated our lips again, I wished him goodnight. I walked into my building, feeling his eyes watching me until I was safely inside.

I did have a slight beer buzz, but not enough to send me to bed. There was work to be done, and now that I had a plan moving forward, I wanted to make sure I didn't let it go. Lubbock wasn't a small place to try and come up with a workable solution, so I sat down at the dining table with the laptop and began thinking of ways and places to stay until someone's goose gets cooked.

Chapter 19

Five days of vacation time was what I ended up asking for, and my timing seemed to be perfect. For one, I told my friends that I craved some alone time after working the night shift tirelessly for months, and everybody agreed they felt the same. When Peg asked me where I was going to spend my time, I told her I wanted to drive to San Diego, touch the ocean, and come back. She first let out a jealous grunt and then told me she wished she could do the same but couldn't due to a lack of available vacation days.

"You're going to come back a new person," she told me when my submission for leave was approved. I thanked her, knowing she had played a big part in getting my application pushed through the director's office. Senior management typically wants a 6-8 week notification before anyone gets leave approved for leave. They always strive to schedule two months ahead of how many people and travel nurses they have each week.

I waited until around Tuesday lunchtime before heading off on my little adventure, a couple of hours after Donnie's plane took off for Reno. A part of me wanted to make sure he wasn't around, perhaps the only person who could have called bullshit on my reasons for applying for Leave. My next scheduled shift wasn't until the following Tuesday anyway, which hopefully gave me more than enough time to work with. I hoped he wouldn't be in a rush to come back and maybe hang around his brother's place for a few extra days.

A backpack and a small suitcase were all I ended up packing, just enough for me to get by with the basics. Although I did raid my pantry for a few snacks, that bag ended up on the passenger side seat beside me when I finally took off and headed north on the 385. The second I reached the city limits and watched the scenery change from urban to country, a kind of heaviness seemed to lift from my shoulders.

Country drives have always been something I have enjoyed ever since I first got my license and the freedom to go with it. Those first few months, I would spend hours out on the state's highways, with nothing but the scenery and the music pumping from my speakers for company. There's something to be said about America's country roads and the serene peace they offer the weary traveler.

State Route 385 took me through to Seminole before changing to the 62, then onto Seagraves, Wellman, and

Brownfield, all the quintessential towns representing the Texan landscape. I found myself unable to wipe the smile from my face. It had been too long since my last drive. It was in Brownfield that I pulled over for some gas and a quick bathroom break before I continued to the final stop on this little day trip.

The grin I'd sported since leaving home disappeared the second I saw the Lubbock City Limits sign, the purpose of my trip washing over me with a vengeance. I pictured Douglas Randall's face watching me enter his domain. A trickle of adrenalin kicked my heartbeat up an extra gear, the anticipation of facing yet another monster spurring me on.

The first thing I did when I finally managed to take a couple of deep breaths and get myself back under control was to head through the city and emerge on State Route 84, which was the direct link between Lubbock and Slaton. I'd booked myself into a nondescript roadside hotel called the Twin Boulder Comfort Inn, the kind with an arch coming off the main building over the driveway that led through to a bunch of rooms all lined up next to each other. The parking spots for each room were positioned at a forty-five-degree angle, and it was right in front of Room 5 that I parked after picking up my key from the reception.

I had researched the place ahead of time and made sure I wouldn't need to provide ID to stay there. I booked online under a fake name and email, paid in cash, and fulfilled my part of the mutually beneficial agreement. They got a couple hundred tax-free dollars, which they didn't need to declare, and I got a room to use as my base while planning a manslaughter...or a dreadful accident if you wanted to go down that route.

The room wasn't anything special, not that I expected it to be so. If anything, the musky smell of age hung in the air, indicating a lack of air circulation, which probably meant that the room wasn't used quite as often as the proprietor might have wanted. A brick wall separated mine from the other rooms, a double mattress ensemble pushed up against one side while a narrow bench ran along the other. A small TV hung off one wall, and beneath it, a bar fridge offered nothing more than an empty ice cube tray. The bathroom had nothing more than a shower with a well-used curtain and a toilet, plus a porcelain sink that featured a cracked corner.

After dropping my bags onto the bed, the first thing I did was carefully check every possible hiding spot for hidden cameras. I didn't fancy myself getting featured on some random porn sites because of a lack of due diligence. I'd heard plenty of horror stories of people who had suffered at the hands of unscrupulous operators, and I wasn't about to go through the same hell.

I first closed all the blinds as best as I could to block out as much light as possible and then turned on my cell phone's flashlight. I used it to check both mirrors, the one in the main room and the one in the bathroom. When both checked out fine, I grabbed a chair and inspected the smoke detector and the base of the ceiling fan, and then worked my way over the television, the ancient-looking DVD player, and the rest of the room. Only when I was absolutely positive, I wasn't being spied on did I move on to the main reason for my stay.

With my laptop in hand, I sat on the bed with my back leaning against the wall and settled in to concentrate on Douglas Randall. While I'd made the decision to travel to Slaton, population 5,600, I still hadn't found a way of disposing of him. Unlike the previous two plans, I'd settled on them quite quickly. Randall proved to be more difficult on account of the lack of access I had to him.

Interestingly enough, he mostly posted on Instagram, and a lot of his posts involved him flaunting his lifestyle to those interested enough to follow him. He'd share pictures of himself eating lavish meals, drinking expensive alcohol, and driving a new car, all paid for with money he'd stolen from the hardworking people he and his cronies intimidated. I even saw a couple of photos of him lying back in a bubble bath, with a champagne flute in hand and some girl massaging his shoulders.

I eventually found one of his close friends on Facebook, a guy with the moniker Austin DeathMetalFan. Austin shared similar posts to Doug, but unlike his friend, he lacked the refinement of wealth to add weight to his posts and wasn't as convincing. From what I could find, he drove a dated F-150 and had a young wife but still insisted on hanging around his friend, hoping to catch any offerings that Doug tossed his way.

What I discovered was that they liked to regularly frequent a bar on the other side of Slaton, the kind of place that measured the success of its night by how much of the furniture remained intact. It was all I had to go on, and given my limited time, I didn't want to waste most of it sitting in a hotel room pondering options. Something I learned pretty quickly in this business was that answers seemed to come faster when out looking for them in person.

I stopped at a drive-through on the way and grabbed myself a burger and fries, plus a chocolate shake. It wasn't that I was hungry, but I knew that this little stakeout might just take longer than expected, especially when I had no idea whether any of the group would even turn up.

The parking lot of Jack's Barrel wasn't exactly filled to the brim when I rolled into the place around seven that night, but there were enough cars to show the popularity of the place, especially considering it was a weeknight. Maybe a dozen cars sat in two rows in the very middle of the lot, with none of them looking familiar to me. Three other vehicles had been parked at the very edge, away from the main group, and I assumed those belonged to the staff. Unlike the majority of his friends who drove pick-up trucks, ole Dougie boy preferred something a lot closer to the ground; his Porsche was probably one of the few German sports cars in the area.

I parked in the far back corner of the parking lot near where the staff parked so I could keep an eye on the front of the building as well as any traffic coming or going from the place. I barely got through half of my burger before a bright yellow F-150 rolled into the lot and parked on my side of the lot. A message buzzed on my phone, and I sent Donnie a quick reply, but not enough to distract me. I held my breath as the headlights went out, and two men climbed out of the cab. Only when they reached the front door, and he slightly turned to look back at his truck, did I recognize Austin DeathMetalFan.

Feeling a lot more hopeful now that I had made the first confirmed sighting of someone related to my target, I began to take more bites of my burger as if feeding the urgency inside me. Each time a subsequent car turned up, I felt a little more adrenalin trickle into my system as I stared open-mouthed at the make of the vehicle, hoping that Randall would show.

Three hours was how long I spent sitting in that parking lot while waiting for him to show, and for three hours, I sat in the hope of getting my first big break. He didn't show, and when Austin walked out of the bar around ten and climbed back into his truck with his buddy, I knew I had a choice to make. Continue waiting for Randall to show up or follow the Ford and see if it would lead me to him instead.

I opted for the latter only because it was a confirmed contact for me. With Austin, a known associate of Douglas "Dougie" Randall, I knew it was far more likely for Austin to lead me than waiting at this establishment. Unfortunately for me, following the F-150 proved to be a bust as well. After dropping his friend off at his house five minutes down the road, the Ford drove on for another five minutes where it pulled into the driveway of another house that turned out to be Austin's home. I could see his wife sitting in the living room through the open window, the light from the television enough to share the room with the outside world.

There didn't appear to be a lot of love between the husband and wife, with one barely acknowledging the other's return. Austin stood in the doorway and said something to her, and she kind of waved him off dismissively before he disappeared from view. I hung around for about thirty more minutes, but I eventually decided to leave when the wife got up, turned off the TV, and then vanished from sight after switching off the lights. It wasn't a failure I'd been expecting, and I knew I had to do better if I was going to succeed.

Chapter 20

The following day proved the same, presenting a series of vague hints and unproductive leads that led me nowhere concrete. Donnie sent me a couple of messages telling me about his day, but we didn't really get into a huge conversation. I felt like a fish out of water, or maybe like some trainee detective, failing her evaluation, trying to find the footsteps. All the things I jotted down before I got here made me rethink this trip. Panic began to set in once I returned to my room around 10 am to regroup my thoughts.

It wasn't all a complete failure. I managed to build a list of a few associates of Douglas Randall, guys who helped him intimidate a few business owners who were funding their lifestyles. One of the places I stopped at was a strip mall made up of several businesses, each suffering regular visits from the group. A hairdresser, a liquor store, a burger place, and a small corner store serving the local community. While a small accountant firm residing in an upstairs unit above the liquor store stood closed. There was also a tattoo parlor, but it looked like it was only available by appointment.

I went inside the burger place and grabbed some lunch. I was soon sitting in my car eating my food while contemplating my next move when the same F-150 rolled into the parking lot. Austin and the other guy climbed out. I watched them walk into the liquor store, make their way behind the counter, and grab the owner by the back of the collar before forcing him to a back room. With nobody else in the store at the time, it was all over within a matter of minutes; then I watched Austin counting the notes on his way back to the truck.

This time, I decided to follow them for as long as I had to. Seeing the way they intimidated the owner of the business fired up a new kind of energy within me, the kind that was beginning to feel a little too familiar. I knew my purpose wasn't to save those businesses or anybody else being held for ransom, but what I hoped for, was to cut the head off the snake. Perhaps the rest of them would quietly disperse.

My determination to get some sort of answers proved to finally pay off when Austin finally arrived at a house in Woodrow, located on the southern side of Lubbock. There were three cars in the driveway, with the white Porsche positioned at the front near the open garage. I felt my insides tighten at the prospect of finally finding the man of the hour.

A group of people sat on the front steps of the house, drinking beers. When Austin and his friend walked up, somebody tossed each of them a can. I'd parked a house over, in between a couple of other cars along the street, and I could barely make out the little gathering from my spot.

The break I'd been looking for ended up taking another hour, but it was time well spent. Just after five, the line of vehicles began to dissipate as each person finished their final drink and headed home. I don't know whose house it was, but it wasn't Doug's. He ended up being the last to leave, and after exchanging a fist bump with the final person left sitting on the steps, he jumped into his car and headed back to the main road.

It wasn't easy following somebody who didn't care about the posted speed limits. He sped through traffic with the same insolence I remembered Kane Nazif displaying, the nonchalant attitude of being above others. I thought I lost him at one point, but ended up catching up again at a perfectly-timed red light.

I followed him all the way to Regal Park, where he pulled into the house's driveway and immediately went inside. Instead of just sitting there staring at the place, hoping for something to happen, I turned my attention to social media to see if I could plan my next move. Five minutes later, the answer came when I opened Facebook and checked Austin's profile. From what I could tell, it was his wife's birthday, and judging by a couple of the posts left on his page, people were planning to catch up with him that night at Jack's Barrel.

Call me stupid, but seeing that post set off a kind of string of ideas in my head. The kind that led me through from conception to execution. With not a lot of time on my hands, I needed a plan that would guarantee success before I had to return to my life in Odessa. At the rate I was going, that was never going to happen. I wouldn't see any change unless I stepped up my game and elevated the stakes.

I can't decide if I devised the plan because I felt overwhelmed by the situation or if I was eager to witness one of these interactions myself. What mattered was the result, and this time, I felt like I needed to take my role to another level. The kind where I took a more… hands-on approach.

I stopped into a nearby liquor store and grabbed a bottle of bourbon, a little something extra I hoped to bring out later that night. After placing the bottle in the back seat, I headed back to the room while thinking about the images Doug had taken of himself in various poses. One of the things that played on my mind was the fact I hadn't seen any indication of Randall getting himself a new girlfriend. None of the pictures his friends posted showed anything either, which opened the door for a plan.

It was time for me to get my hands dirty and handle one of the abusers directly. Not wanting to get to Jack's too early, I took my time getting ready, all while wondering how I would pull off the impossible. My goal was simple, get close enough to Randall to deliver...something special. I hadn't exactly packed an abundant number of outfits and had to work with what I had, but I figured it was worth a shot. If I failed, then I could always regroup and live to fight another day.

The first thing I did was take a shower, followed by drying my hair using the hotel's provided hairdryer. Knowing I might need some kind of disguise, I took out the wig I had bought a month ago and thought about whether I really wanted to wear it. One look in the mirror was enough for me to decide, I did. Why forego using an advantage and risk getting caught, right?

When I finished applying my makeup, I slipped into some masterpiece jeans and a t-shirt. The jeans had an artistic design that women sometimes have spray-painted on. Talk about snug. When I checked myself in the mirror, I could see why they were designed that way. These pants serve the single purpose of drawing attention...or to my butt, anyway.

By the time I finished getting ready and checked myself in the mirror again, the person gazing back at me looked anything but myself. A stranger's face, wearing makeup beyond my own preferences, and sporting a vivid hair color that perfectly complemented the look. It was an unsettling sight, yet there was a strange thrill in that darkness that drew me in.

I waited until almost nine before heading out again, figuring that it would give the party plenty of time to get going. I ordered a cab and again paid cash to keep the transaction from any databases. I knew the boys would likely be bored with their female partners, and many would solve this by having a few extra drinks to numb the discomfort. If Douglas Randall was as good of a friend as he made it out to be, then maybe he would stick around long enough for me to work my magic. Or at least that was the plan.

My aim was to get there, find a quiet corner, and assess the situation from a difference. It almost worked out that way, were it not for the overzealous patron sitting at the bar who decided to pay me a little too much attention from the moment he spotted me. I could smell the stale beer on his breath even over the bar's general alcoholic fragrance, but I did my best to ignore it as I ordered a rum and coke.

"Pretty lady like you shouldn't drink alone," the guy said to me as he leaned a little closer toward me.

"It's OK, I have someone coming," I told him, and the second the bartender brought me my drink, I disappeared to one of the booths.

To my dismay, I hadn't seen Randall's Porsche in the parking lot, but he didn't appear to be sitting with his friends who took up the main tables. This segregated area near the back is the kind of half-enclosed room allocated to parties. Two tables, each with ten chairs, were almost all filled up with the couples. I saw Austin and his wife, plus a few other faces I've come across in social media posts, but no Randall.

"It doesn't look like your friend is showing," a voice suddenly said from beside me. When I looked up, I saw the same guy from the bar who was now hoping to sit next to me.

"He'll be here," I said, adding a hint of frustration to my tone.

"Why you got to be unsociable like that, sweetheart," the guy said. I would have given him credit for his dedication, but that was when he took things too far. "Go on, shove aside, and I'll share a drink with ya," he said as he set his glass next to mine, leaned down, and tried to push me further into the booth with his side. During the struggle, he spilled his drink, and when he tried to catch his glass, he also knocked mine over.

"Damn it," he said as he swiped the glasses off the table in disgust. He began pulling his other hand back in preparation to swing it at me, but that was when someone caught his arm and pulled him clean off the chair.

"What the -" was all the drunk managed to squawk before I watched him suddenly get half-dragged toward the door. In his place, a face looked down at me. At any other moment, it might have captured my interest in more than a flattering way, especially given the warmth of the smile behind it.

"Are you alright? Reg tends to become a bit too rowdy after a few drinks," Douglas Randall remarked while he wiped up the spilled drinks from the table with some napkins. "Don't worry, my friends will make sure he won't come back in and bother you."

"Thank you," I said, doing my best to hide the shock of seeing him.

"Haven't seen you around here before. You new in town?"

"You could say that."

"Well, not the sort of welcome we usually offer strangers." He held out a hand to me, and we shook, his demeanor a complete surprise to me. "I'm Doug."

"Ellie."

"Well, hello, Ellie. My friends and I are having a little party over there. Care to join us?"

"Actually, I'd rather not, if that's OK. Had kind of a shit day." He immediately held both hands up in a kind of surrender.

"Nope, that's quite alright. Just thought I'd ask."

He ended up wishing me a good night, and just like he said, he headed to where his friends were waiting and joined the group. I watched on just as I had promised myself, occasionally ordering drinks but making sure to keep them non-alcoholic. From where I was sitting, I could see the boredom on the faces of the boys as they had to remain on their best behavior for their partners. Because of this, a lot more alcohol flowed, and I could see the intoxication increase exponentially as the night wore on. Even Randall loaded up, and when it looked like he had consumed more than enough, out came the persona I knew to be hiding just under the skin.

First, he picked a fight with one of the women sitting at the other table. I couldn't quite make out what the fight was over, but they got pretty heated, and the words thrown between them were quite venomous. It ended up fiery enough for the woman to grab her purse and demand her boyfriend or husband to drive her home. He, unfortunately, didn't know which way to go with both combatants staring at him to see where his loyalties lay. When he opted to follow his wife out the door, Randall shouted a couple of final insults after him and then sat there grinning to himself.

And that was when he spotted me again. Figuring he'd take his chances with the stranger who shouldn't have known his dark side, Randall got to his feet, grabbed his glass, and came back to where our initial introductions had taken place just a couple of hours earlier. This time, the attempted charm fell flat.

"You know it's considered rude for a town to leave a guest drinking alone," as he sat on the opposite side of the booth. Bloodshot eyes gazed across the table at me, his head hanging low as if too heavy for him. That was when I knew it was time to strike.

"You know, it's considered rude not to invite a girl home after making her wait all night," I whispered to him, and his eyes immediately lit up with hope.

"I don't know about going home, but they have rooms here. How about I get us one?"

"Sure," I said, feeling my insides knot up into a bundle of nerves.

While watching Randall walk to the side of the bar and speak with one of the waitresses, I wondered which of my emotions I found the hardest to deal with. The fear, the nervousness, the dread, the anticipation, they all intermingled into a mass of confusion I tried my best to push down into the pit of my stomach.

Randall turned around and held up a key, dangling it from his fingers while wearing the biggest grin. I grabbed my purse and slid out from the booth, doing my best to keep my face away from the only security camera I'd seen fixed in one of the corners. The wig helped me plenty, and I was pretty confident I'd done enough to conceal my identity.

We left the bar area, climbed a set of stairs, and walked down a long corridor, all while there was a hand groping my butt. I couldn't bear the touch of him but knew there was no turning back. If I was going to go through with my plan, this would have to be something I worked through.

"Damn, I'm going to take my time with you," he tried to whisper into my ear when we reached the door to our room, but he belched halfway through, and the stink of his breath just about caused me to take a step back. Randall didn't notice, more interested in my bust line as he fumbled the keys into the lock, another job he was completely incapable of performing.

"Here, let me," I said, grabbed the keys, and opened the door.

Once inside and with the door safely locked, I led Randall to the bed and pulled out my little backup plan.

"Listen, why don't you start on this, and I'll go and freshen up a bit, OK?"

I held up the bourbon and swung it from side to side in front of his face.

"I like my men nice and relaxed,"

Then, to question his manhood, I added, "You can drink this straight, can't you? My last boyfriend could down one of these with no problems."

"Gimme that, I'll put him to shame," Randall mumbled, untwisted the top, and took a swig.

While I walked to the door, Randall took a couple more mouthfuls, and just before I closed the door to the bathroom, I could see him contemplating the rest of it.

"Won't be long," I told him and closed the door.

Careful to leave the wig on, I stripped off my t-shirt and jeans and set them aside on top of the toilet. Next, I began to run the bath, making sure to keep the water just above body temperature. I didn't want it to be too hot or too cold, but just at the point where a person would feel it the least. Only when the bath was three-quarters full did I shut off the faucet and turn my attention back to the room.

Wearing just my underwear, I swallowed hard, took a deep breath, and opened the door. What I hoped to find was Randall passed out on the bed, the monster subdued to the point where I could carry out what I needed without facing too much resistance. If he wasn't, then I would have to figure out how to proceed without having to strip down any further, something I definitely wasn't prepared to go through.

He wasn't on the bed, nor was he passed out. While taking a drink from the bottle, he leaned back a little too far and rolled off the side of the bed. Randall was lying on the floor and mumbling something about wanting to take me to heaven while fumbling with the zipper of his jeans. I could tell he was way beyond ordinary intoxication, and with enough time, sleep wouldn't be too far away.

"Why don't I help you with that," I said as I knelt down beside him and pulled his hand away from his fly.

"Oh, yeah, baby, you do it," he managed to mumble, although the final few syllables barely rose from his lips.

I slowly popped the button and pulled the zipper down. My thumb brushed the side of his manhood, and I was surprised he could still get it up, considering the amount of alcohol in his system. As I pulled his boots off and then his socks, Randall kept trying to tell me what he was going to do to me, but the alcohol worked against him, each passing second robbing him of more strength.

By the time I finally pulled his shirt off, Randall lay on the floor wearing just his underwear. His eyes had already closed, unaware that they would soon never see daylight again. He did have enough strength to help me get him to the bathroom, but when he flopped on the tiles and rolled onto his side, I knew I would need to get him into the tub myself.

The light snoring began almost the instant he stopped mumbling, the sounds echoing in the small room as I maneuvered him the rest of the way. I didn't think I had the strength to get him into it, but it's amazing how much a person can do when truly committed. All I had to do was remember the images of the women he'd hurt, and it was enough to propel me forward. As a final bit of poetic justice, I opened my cell phone and brought up the video of Renee Ross. The nineteen-year-old whom he brutalized in many ways. Before I pulled him into the tub, It was her crying he would have heard just before he sank into the water.

I watched Douglas Randall in those final moments, the sobbing of his girlfriend playing to keep him company. There wasn't much of a fight left in him. After holding him to the bottom of the tub, he opened his eyes just enough to gaze into mine. After some struggle and kicking, his time ran out. I'd like to think that he knew what was happening and why, that he heard the cries of a woman representing the many he'd beaten during his time on earth.

That was the first time I had committed an act that was considered murder. I had rolled with a few ideas that night, prepared a killing, and then executed the plan with lethal precision. While I could have described the others as nothing more than accidents, this time, that was no longer the case. I had stepped over the line and murdered an abuser, and for that, I would pay.

Chapter 21

The only word I can use to describe the feeling that ravaged me once I confirmed that Douglas Randall had died was panic. It gripped me harder and faster than anything I could have imagined possible. At first, my fight-or-flight instincts nearly caused me to run straight out the door, but that sensation quickly passed when I imagined the reaction of his friends, who would no doubt still be sitting down in the bar area.

My next instinct to kick in was self-preservation, and having spent at least a half hour in the room already, I knew my DNA would already be all over the place. I began to rub down every single surface I could, including the door handles, the faucets, the mirror, the walls, the entire bathtub area, and anything else I deemed necessary. Next, I went to work on the clothes, meticulously wiping Randall's boots, the button on his jeans, the zipper, the bottle, and the belt buckle.

The truth is, I couldn't remember everything I had touched, and in my panicked state, I figured it best to wipe down absolutely everything, including that room key. I hadn't kissed the guy, nor let him touch me per se, which meant it was doubtful that any of me would be found on his fingers. When I paused in the bathroom and once again saw my reflection in the mirror, I thought about the wig. It probably saved me from dropping any of my own hairs in the room, but could the same for rogue eyelashes or the fine body hairs people shed every minute of the day?

Believe it or not, my sense of self-preservation became so strong that I considered setting a fire in the room and running before it entirely took hold. I even looked at the bed sheets and considered using them for fuel but quickly dismissed the idea when I thought about anyone else staying in adjoining rooms. If anybody else got hurt, I don't think I could have lived with myself. This was between Douglas Randall and Fate and nobody else.

I remember hearing about a celebrity drowning in the tub due to substance abuse. Although I couldn't remember exactly who it was, I did recall something about the water being hot enough to hide the time of death. Rolling the idea over in my mind, I looked through the doorway to where I could see the edge of the bathtub, wondering if Randall was continuing to enjoy his introduction to the afterlife. Did I really want to cook him?

I don't know whether it was the right call, but the one thing I learned early on was to always follow one's instincts, and this time, they told me to turn on the hot water faucet. Slowly walking back into the bathroom, I stood next to the tub and stared down into those half-open eyes, the ones now looking completely devoid of that spark living people displayed.

To try and buy myself a little extra time, I reached into the water, pushed my hand between the feet, and pulled out the plug. I waited until the water level dropped to almost half before plugging it up again. Grabbing a handful of toilet paper to save me leaving yet more fingerprints, I turned on the hot water faucet until the water was running, but not forcefully. I didn't want to cause a flood within the first ten minutes. What I needed was time to make my escape.

Before walking out of the bathroom for the final time, I took a last look into the tub, where the ripples caused Randall's face to quiver beneath the waves. I wondered whether he felt anything during his final few moments or if the alcohol had shown him the mercy he so didn't deserve, the compassion he never showed any of his victims.

"Sorry, not sorry," was what I said to him, and that was how I left the man who became the fourth person I've delivered justice to.

Only after making thoroughly sure that I'd wiped down every surface and grabbed all of my things to put them on before I dared to walk toward the door. With the wig still attached, I tried to keep my head down enough for some of the hair to fall over my face and shield myself from any possible cameras.

Once out in the hallway, I didn't dare hesitate. Instead of walking back the way we had come earlier, I continued down the rest of the corridor, turned the corner at the end, and found the Fire Escape. It opened up at the back of the building, the opposite end to the parking lot, and not a place bathed in lights.

During my brief research of the place, I found that the bar backed onto the barren wasteland that was outback Texas. I wasn't a stranger to walking, so I began the long walk back to the hotel under the cover of darkness. For the next three hours, all I had for company was the moon above and the traffic driving along Route 84, although that began to thin out the longer I spent walking through the night.

The one thing I did was dispose of the wig somewhere during that excursion through the darkness. Half a mile further along, I tossed the bourbon bottle. My jeans went shortly after that, and I put on the skirt I'd packed for myself. By the time I made it back to the hotel at around four that morning, the only things I still had on from the bar were my shoes and those I ended up taking with me and tossing out of the car some twenty miles apart while driving down a couple of lonely country roads.

I didn't drive home, not right then anyway. I needed time away, time to give myself a chance to come to terms with what I've done. I wish I could tell you that the drive did wonders for me, but the truth is that the miles I passed mattered little. Grief, guilt, whatever it was, the pain running through me proved much too powerful to resist, and by three that afternoon, I had to give in.

Albuquerque was how far I ended up making it before I ran out of steam. The urge for me to scream came on about as suddenly as someone fighting a bear. I ended up pulling to the side of the road, gripping the steering wheel as tightly as I could, and just let it out. Torment tore through me as my insides expelled the guilt-ridden fear, burning fingers scraping the inside of my throat. I don't know how long I sat there trying to rip the steering wheel free, my hands pulling it back and forth as the screams continued until nothing but a shrill screeching came out. And yet no tears fell. No, those would wait for a more private moment.

Only when I was sure I had somewhat of a hold over my emotions did I dare pull back out onto the road again. A few miles further down, I found a roadside hotel and quickly checked in with the last of the cash I had. I didn't think it would have mattered much using my credit card, but then again, I didn't put too much thought into it.

When I walked into that first hotel room that Saturday afternoon, I collapsed back onto the door after closing it and began sobbing uncontrollably as the tears finally arrived. The mind-numbing nerves that had ravaged my soul since the moment I left Jack's Barrel some nine hours earlier finally won their battle, and the vomitous tears flowed the second I felt hidden enough from the world.

I don't remember getting myself off the floor, nor climbing into bed, but that was where I ended up because I woke up in total darkness, however long later. The panic returned as it took me a few moments to remember exactly where I was. Only when I noticed the outer edge of the blinds lit up by a light outside my room did I get a vague memory of the hotel.

My cell phone still sat in my pocket, and when I pulled it out, I found it having just 3% battery power left, just enough for me to read the message Donnie sent me a few hours earlier.

I didn't let on that there was anything wrong, and he didn't ask, so I just kind of let it go. I know I probably acted completely disinterested in him, and I guess, in a way I was.

How often does a straight-laced girl go out and kill a man?

"You removed a nuisance of society," I whispered to myself as the phone beeped at me, signaling that I was about to lose power, and I shut it off before going over to my bag to grab my cord.

After a quick detour to the bathroom, complete with a spinal shiver, when I spotted the tub, I set up the charger and left the phone sitting on the bed beside me. I laid on the bed for a few minutes listening to the distant hum of traffic out on the interstate and wondered whether or not they'd already sent out detectives looking for someone responsible for the death of Douglas Randall.

Surprisingly, I fell back to sleep just a few minutes after shutting off the light and ended up enduring one of the most nightmarish periods of sleep in living history. If I didn't know better, I would have guessed that my latest victim had discovered the secret to interdimensional revenge because that night, he murdered me over and over again in my sleep.

Chapter 22

While Douglas Randall's death didn't make national news, it did feature on a number of websites as well as news bulletins. Reports mentioned that a mystery girl had been previously seen in the company of the well-respected young man. Law enforcement is asking for any witnesses to come forward to help with their investigation of the unfortunate incident.

Butterflies began to soar in my stomach the moment I saw the first report, but I didn't settle again until I watched the last of the news bulletins. They did share the bar's security footage, but not only did it look like it had been filmed by a potato, but the only two shots appeared to be from behind us walking down the corridor toward the room and one of the parking lot of me arriving by taxi.

I couldn't believe that it was me they were talking about.

Me..., the dedicated, hard-working, reliable nurse from Odessa who'd never had so much as a parking ticket in her life and now suddenly found herself responsible for four deaths.

Me, who once cried for three straight hours after running over an innocent cat that had ran straight out in front of my car and ended up suffering just a broken leg.

When I climbed back into my car that Sunday morning and began heading out of Albuquerque, I honestly felt like I was running. No, not just running, but running in the wrong direction. The intense guilt coursing through me felt obnoxiously surreal, almost as if I'd been playing a small part in a movie and now found myself thrust into the lead role without a script.

I don't think I had ever felt a greater need to be home than I did at that moment. My apartment, my safe place, seven hours away...that was where I knew I could get my brain in order and sort the mess out. I swung my little car around so fast that a mile down the road, I questioned whether I actually did or didn't do it. After driving the next four miles with my mouth hung open, I waited for the next road sign indicating my direction. Thank goodness I was heading in the right direction.

A text came through from Peg asking how my vacation was going and another from Donnie asking if I was alright. I couldn't respond for almost fifty miles, and only then, after pulling into a random truck stop, did I keep my distance from everyone in case somebody recognized me. I told Peg that I was just fine and heading home, and Donnie...well, I wasn't sure about what to say to him, so since he was back, I asked whether he wanted to come around that night for pizza. His acceptance came through barely ten seconds later, another sign of just how keen he was on me.

Something about communicating with friends seemed to settle me, and the drive home didn't feel quite as bad after that. When I walked through my door hours later, it almost felt like I had made the entire thing up in my head...almost. Relief did wash over me in a faint and fragile kind of way while dropping my bags onto the bed, and then, that safe feeling returned, the one that came from familiar surroundings, but that niggling guilt remained in the shadows.

It still clung to my conscience a couple of hours later when I opened the door after a knock and was temporarily piqued during the kiss-and-hug greeting between Donnie and me but then faded again when we sat out on the balcony with our beer and pizza. We talked while we ate, him sharing his trip and me pretending to remember what he'd texted me so far. The tricky thing about lying about your work week is that it's pure fantasy and challenging to remember, so I tried to keep the details to a minimum. Of course, he noticed.

"Are you sure everything is alright, Liz? You seem awfully distant," he asked me once we both agreed to forego the final slice, and I closed the box to stop myself from picking off the toppings.

"I'm just tired, that's all," I said, and to try to deflect the conversation, I held up my empty bottle and offered him a fresh one.

I took the two empty bottles and the box back to the kitchen, grabbed a couple of fresh beverages from the fridge, and went to take them back outside, but as I turned, I found Donnie standing right behind me. I half-walked into him, and when I looked up to apologize, he leaned down and pressed his lips onto mine.

The kiss happened so suddenly that for the briefest moment, I didn't react. It should have been nice, perhaps one of those pivotal moments in a relationship, and maybe it was, just not in the way he might have expected. I cringed, pulled back, and while trying to push myself off him, I dropped one of the beer bottles. It hit the floor hard, smashed into a thousand pieces, and rained ice-cold booze over my bare feet.

"Oh shit," I cried out as the explosion of glass echoed through the kitchen, broken shards tinkering across the floor. Donnie looked more pained than surprised, and I immediately felt another wave of guilt rush over me.

"Eliza, I'm sorry if I -"

"No, please," I said, went to take a step back, but he grabbed my hand to stop me.

"Don't, there's glass everywhere. Here." He leaned down, and before I could resist, he picked me off the floor and sat me on the bench. "Stay there for a second."

"Donnie, really, I can get it," I said and stupidly went to slide off the bench, but that was when he snapped at me.

"Damn it", Liz, is it that difficult having me help you?" His words cut through the air like tiny daggers, each carrying a hint of venom as if in retaliation. I felt terrible, not just for the kiss but also for the way I made him feel.

"I just...I just want to clean up," I said, now feeling like I needed to defend myself. From what exactly, I didn't know, but it didn't go well for me.

"Fine," Donnie said, the frustration even more evident in his tone. "I'll leave you to it."

Before I could say another word, he turned and walked out of the apartment, the door closing with a sharp thump that echoed his exasperation.

"Donnie, wait," I called out after him, but the words came out too late, and I ended up sitting on that bench listening to the cold silence while engulfed by the heavy scent of beer.

"Great, absolutely great," I mumbled to myself and eventually spun myself to the opposite side of the bench, put on my shoes, and started to look around where the glass had landed. It didn't take me too long to clean up the mess I'd made, a quick sweep and mop taking care of the physical damage. Cleaning up the unknown glass shards would eventually show themselves. The mental damage I'd caused Don wasn't as easy to fix, and he was already ignoring the first text I sent him. I even tried asking whether he wanted to come back and try for dessert. I guess humor wasn't exactly my forte, and when he still hadn't answered by nine that night, I figured I'd let him simmer down on his own.

I guess I should have taken the hint and just gone to bed myself. The day had been a lengthy one for me, and the fatigue weighed me down long before I got back into my apartment. Yet I tried everything to avoid sleep. Maybe because of the previous nightmare or just the thought of things catching up with me, I couldn't bring myself to give in to the tiredness.

The plan was to lie in bed and put on a movie, something super boring that I'd quickly lose interest in, and then fall asleep. Instead, I found myself channel surfing and then scrolling through some of the social media platforms on my second phone. I should have known to leave things alone, but the curiosity won me over.

I barely got the Facebook app open before I came across multiple posts about Douglas Randall. His friends had all posted about their grief and how he didn't deserve to go out that way. That is something I'm pretty certain was up for debate. Several mentioned the red-haired girl who had accompanied him into the room that night, and it was when one of them left a comment on one of the posts that my blood turned cold.

No way that red hair was real was what a girl named Taryn Baxter wrote in her comment. Several people liked it, and one other reacted to it. That wasn't the only thing fake about her; someone else responded, but that was as far as I got before I swiped the app closed, shut off the phone, and tossed it on the bed.

The nerves I'd fought so hard to overcome came flooding back, the reality of my actions blowing up in that moment. I began to shake, my fingers trembling enough to prevent me from picking up the phone to put on the nightstand. I closed my eyes to try to control my breathing. Unlike the previous deaths that had simply gone away on their own, I could sense that this one wasn't doing the same, and if I waited long enough, someone was going to piece together the clues and find the girl responsible.

Chapter 23

I tried to return to my life as best I could, but the fear and nerves were never far away. Work ended up being a kind of saving grace for me, not just because I could lose myself in the hustle and bustle of the ED. But also, because I found myself surrounded by friends and colleagues, people who knew and respected me. They were also the people who would have never suspected me capable of such heinous crimes, and in a way, it was their lack of understanding that gave me a false sense of security, something I could hide behind when not faced with the realities of my inner self.

Fortunately for me, the investigation into Douglas Randall's passing was eventually ruled as death by misadventure by the coroner, which meant that despite questions remaining about the way he died, there wasn't a greater focus on trying to find someone else responsible. Randall's own actions, namely him drinking himself stupid as he had done on countless prior occasions, were what ultimately led to him drowning in a tub. The red-haired girl was seen as a person of interest, but I don't know whether law enforcement made her a priority in their ongoing duties.

That left me to deal with the psychological repercussions of my own actions, and while the guilt did ravage me, the video of Renee Ross always helped out whenever I felt a need to remind myself of why I drove to Slaton in the first place. It was the part about ending the suffering of victims that always managed to make me feel better, and when I didn't get a knock on the door from some overly invested detective after almost a month, I knew that Fate had stepped in once more to help me.

Time didn't just heal me, but also the relationship between Donnie and me. It took him a few days to simmer down, but once he did, he texted me every day until I finally offered him a second pizza night at my place. This time, when he leaned in to kiss me, I didn't resist, and for the first time in like forever, I felt that tingle rush through my body.

I think if Fate had stepped away at that point and considered my job finished, I could have happily gone on with the rest of my life, satisfied that I had done my part to help women in need. Four was a good number to retire on, four abusive men taken out of the world to never harm helpless victims again. Unfortunately, destiny had other ideas for me, and it was during a night shift in early April that fate came knocking once more.

It was Peg who spoke the words that I had been dreading just before nine that Friday night, words I had envisioned multiple times and always shuddered away from.

"Eliza, DV in Room 3 for you," she told me in passing, and that was how I came to meet Laurie Sumner, a woman who would forever change the course of so many lives.

Just before I opened the door to go inside, I felt something inside me twitch enough to give me a reason to pause, my hand on the door handle held in mid-swing once again. It wasn't dread or anticipation or even nerves that I felt. It kind of felt like... finality. I could sense that whatever was waiting for me on the other side of the door would affect my entire future, and there was nothing I could do about it. After a deep breath, I forced myself to turn the handle the rest of the way and went inside.

Laurie Sumner shocked me when I first laid eyes on her; the woman was barely able to see me through the purplish swelling running along the top of her face. A piece of her scalp had been torn off, and the paramedics were still with her, unstrapping her from the stretcher. Working my eyes down the face, her nose hooked severely to the left, a sure sign it was broken, and her cut-up lips parted each time she moaned to reveal teeth broken at the gum line.

It was clear she'd need surgery and lots of it, and that was just my assessment from looking at her without an examination. The first thing I did was try to reassure her that everything was going to be alright, that whatever happened, she was safe and going to get the care she needed. The poor thing shivered from the volume of trauma her body had taken and put on such a brave face, but I knew this wasn't some one-off assault. Whoever had done this to her didn't care about repercussions or anybody asking questions.

Dr. Raj was the one who came in to assess the patient properly and, as well as all the facial injuries, added a couple of broken ribs and a fractured thumb to the list. The beating came close to claiming one of her eyes, if not her life, and the worst part was that she had three young children at home. If anybody needed the kind of help I had considered giving up providing, it was this woman.

Laurie Sumner didn't stay in the ED for long. Once the doctor finished her assessment, she was prioritized for surgery and underwent what can only be described as facial reconstruction; the severity of the injuries was not fully known until X-rays revealed the reality. She remained in surgery for more than eight hours, requiring plates to be screwed onto her skull to keep it together. It was lucky the woman survived at all.

I made sure to visit with her at the start and end of each of my subsequent shifts, always hoping to run into the man who caused such extensive injuries. The thing is, after the whole

Douglas Randall thing, I wasn't sure whether I was cut out for doing what I thought I was chosen for. That, along with the ongoing fear of still getting picked up for questioning over the Slaton incident.

What made matters worse was what I initially thought was just my own insecurities continuously taunting me. It really came to the forefront during a brunch I'd organized for Donnie and me out at The Silver Lining early one Sunday morning. The place had begun serving breakfast only the month before, and I'd heard several of the other girls rave about it, so I wanted to try it for myself.

The establishment had also built a brand new deck, and we got to try it out ourselves, sitting there on that gorgeous morning, enjoying the bright sunshine with a gentle breeze to keep the temperatures down. We both ordered the Easy Hashbrown Breakfast Casserole and shared the Bacon Strata, and I have to admit, it was incredible, definitely worth the effort of getting our butts out of bed.

The issue arose after we'd finished our food and were enjoying a cappuccino. Donnie and I had been making small talk, so to speak, chatting about nothing in particular, when he made the comment that would change the course of the morning for me.

"You know they built this deck over the spot where that guy died last year." That comment caught me off guard, and I nearly spat out the sip of coffee I'd just taken. Feeling a sudden surge of responsibility, I could feel my body go numb, and I think I tried to hide behind the cup.

"Oh, really?"

"Yeah, I heard the owner freaked out over it and relocated the loading dock around to the side," Donnie continued, pointing to the corner of the building. And that was when he said something that sent the hairs on the back of my neck to attention. "Weren't you and your friends here that night?"

"I'm sorry, what?" The question caught me entirely off guard.

"I swear I remember seeing you here. It was how I recognized you at the hospital."

"I wasn't here that night," I said before considering my answer. Inside, I immediately kicked myself for such a stupid mistake. Why the hell would I lie about such a thing when there was no reason to?

"Are you sure? I could have sworn you and a couple of your friends were here."

"I'm not sure, maybe we were," I said, trying to back pedal my answer. "We do come here often."

I don't know why, but a part of me felt that Donnie didn't just ask the question to make conversation. Something felt off about the exchange of questions, and yet I couldn't put my finger on why. He dismissed the conversation almost as quickly as he brought it up, changing the direction of our talk to another cafe he wanted to take me to for brunch since I'd organized this one.

"Maybe we could make it a regular outing, this brunch thing," he said with a grin. He took a gulp of coffee, finished his cup, and ordered another.

While our conversation didn't go back to the vicinity of Brian Hurst or the unfortunate accident he'd suffered on a now-removed loading dock, I did feel the air between us remain at the same suspicious level, or at least it did for me. I couldn't help but wonder why he would bring up the incident in the first place, but more than that, I couldn't understand why he would pretend to have been there when I knew for a fact he wasn't.

Chapter 24

When Laurie Sumner left the hospital three weeks after arriving in a battered state, she did so with the knowledge she would be returning to the exact same situation she had been in when she arrived. My own problems battling my consciousness and guilt didn't strictly subside either, or at least not enough for me to start seriously considering investigating her life. The only information I had on the woman was the details I gained from processing her that first night which really only gave me her current address and next of kin.

I was there that morning, having made it my business to check on her before she was wheeled out of those doors. It was also during that exchange when I asked her if she really wanted to allow herself to go back to a man who'd beaten her so viciously. I'd taken over control of the wheelchair from the assigned nurse, who happily handed the patient over to me.

"Bailey's fine when he's not drinking," was what she told me in the elevator as we headed down to the ground floor. Laurie never provided any specific details, but she pretty much pointed it out. Her words were almost as shocking as the scar running down the edge of her face that she tried to hide with her long brown hair.

I thought to myself, it seems like all of us hide behind our hair...

Anyway, it wasn't the words that convinced me she wouldn't make any changes, but instead, it was her tone. One that sounded so weak and defeated, almost apologizing for her partner's actions. I didn't make it obvious that her words stunned me, nor did I give her any indication of my own disgusted feelings. Up until that moment, I maintained a certain level of patient-nurse interaction, speaking the way any regular colleague of mine would have. If I'm being honest, I still hadn't made the decision to intervene at all, not in a committed kind of way.

If I hadn't seen who was picking her up, things may have turned out quite differently, but seeing him, I did, and immediately felt myself drawn into a matter. I'd only been toying with myself until then. This guy rolled up in a beaten-up Dodge Durango that looked like it hadn't been washed this century. He pulled up alongside the curb, jumped out, and immediately hollered out to his girlfriend.

"Let's go, let's go," he shouted at Laurie with impatience as he opened the passenger door.

"Alright, I have to get going now," she whispered to me, forced a smile, and pushed herself out of the chair.

This dude refused to move, and neglected to assist Laurie with the bag she was carrying. He didn't offer to help her into the vehicle, and he didn't close the door after she got in. Instead, he kept looking over at me with that same contemptuous expression as if waiting for me to say something. If I did, I had little doubt he would have charged at me like a raging bull and turned me into pulp.

Just seeing him sent chills through me, his musclebound arms stretching the edges of the t-shirt to their limits. Tattoos covered every visible bit of skin, encircling both arms, his chest, neck, and the sides of his face. His shaved head also featured a couple, but none of them were what drew my attention. It was those cold, heartless eyes staring back at me that chilled the blood in my veins.

He held my gaze for an extra few seconds as if trying to intimidate me before returning to the driver's side. Once inside, he started the engine, revved it to the extreme a couple of times, and then took off with tires squealing, leaving behind nothing but a thick cloud of smoke. That was the first time I saw him, but in my mind, I already knew it wouldn't be the last. If ever I saw a real monster capable of destroying lives, it was this guy, Bailey, especially after seeing his aftermath.

When I got back to my apartment that morning, I went to work almost the instant I walked through the door. The chills from seeing those eyes still hadn't quite dissipated, and when I opened my laptop, I found my fingers visibly shaking, not from fear for myself, but for Laurie. I didn't want to imagine what she'd be going through at this very moment, but that was exactly what kept giving me intrusive thoughts.

The biggest problem I had was that I still didn't have a full name for this Bailey guy responsible for Laurie's injuries. She'd given me her mother's name as her next of kin, and when asked about her relationship status, she told me she was divorced. Logic states she lived a restricted lifestyle, and apparently, family members were limited. The only genuine leads I had were a Dodge Durango, and the address that she left on file.

I figured my best chance of putting a full name to that face was to get ahold of hospital security. They had cameras at all entrances and corners of the hospital. After all, I didn't get a direct view of his license plate because of how he parked and how he exited stage right.

After a quick visit to security to see Cliff, he was able to zoom in on the plate and provide me the number. Since the hospital was a private company, they were unable to handle any city matters regarding reckless driving. Nevertheless, hospital staff members would receive a parking ticket for not parking in the designated employee lot. Most of the employees believed it was a lose-lose situation.

What helped me was knowing exactly the kind of car the man drove, thanks to my coworker who owned the exact same model a few years back. Using the information I had, I decided that the best way for me to get the breakthrough I needed was to swindle my way forward. So I did the only thing possible, I phoned the Lee County Tax office. It was the place that handled registration renewals, license plates, and of course, title transfers, and I intended to try to use it to my advantage.

I dialed the number to the office and swallowed hard to try and suppress the anxiety away. It began to ring almost immediately and two seconds later, a pleasant woman's voice greeted me.

"Good morning, Lee County Tax Office, Shirley speaking."

"Good morning," I said, using the most pleasant house-wifey tone I could conjure.

"Shirley, my name is Hillary, and I was hoping you could help me."

Shirley said, "Yes, of course,"

"I'd just like to make sure my husband registered the papers for a vehicle he's just bought for our eldest son. Could you do that? I know Trevor gets so forgetful at times."

"Yes, certainly. May I have the make and model of the car as well as the license plate details?"

"Of course, it's a 2001 Dodge Durango," followed by the plate's details. I could hear the keystrokes in the background as the woman typed them into her system. It took her a few moments, which felt like an eternity to me, as I hoped my plan would work.

Shirley said, "The vehicle's registration was updated a couple of months ago, Is that how long ago you purchased it?"

"Yeah, about a few months ago."

"And is your son's name Bailey Saunders?"

"Bailey, yes, that's our boy. Thank you so much for your help, Shirley."

"Would you like to confirm your address so I can make sure the --Click--" That was as much as I heard before I ended the call. It wasn't exactly a question I wanted to answer. I did feel a little remorseful hanging up on her, considering how pleasant she had been, but that's just the nature of the beast.

Bailey Saunders. I finally had the name of the sadistic piece of shit who now had my full attention. Feeling my insides just about double up, I typed the name into Google and pressed enter, and the instant the results filled my screen, I knew I had a challenge ahead of me. Instead of social media links that appeared for most names searched, what I saw were endless news articles, all featuring the name I'd put in, right alongside terms such as assault, injuries, and the one that caused my heart to skip a beat...murder.

I questioned how long they had been together or whether Laurie was aware of who she was dating or possibly living with. I highly doubt she would have gone along with it if she'd known he was a convicted murderer.

The first news article I read reported that Bailey had killed a man by beating him to death during a brutal bar fight in Fort Worth. He was convicted of second-degree murder because he initially knocked down the victim, Malik Zayed, walked away, and then returned to strike him again while he was on the ground. The article was dated March 2016.

The next page I clicked on followed the trial in more depth, but it didn't bring up anything new for me. The third article, however, jumped ahead by several years. This statement shares the disgust of Malik Zayed's family about the killer's release due to a technicality. The article mentioned something about a critical piece of evidence that wasn't presented in court, and the defense counsel argued it would have shed new light on the case. A subsequent retrial found Saunders not guilty, and he won himself an immediate release.

That article was dated November of the previous year, which meant Saunders had been back out in the community for several months. He's had plenty of time to get to know his victim and begin terrorizing her and her family. I checked several more articles, but aside from a couple of other assault charges, the articles just kept going back to the retrial.

I don't know why I had a sudden urge to see Laurie Sumner's house for myself at that moment. But before I knew it, I'd packed the laptop up, grabbed my phone, purse, and keys, and headed out into the day. Twenty minutes later, I found myself parked halfway down a fairly common suburban block, staring at a corner house with a distinctive Dodge Durango parked out front.

The home itself looked well maintained, complete with a luscious garden filled with all sorts of colors. Laurie stood near the front fence with a hose in hand, watering a few of her flowers. She wore a large straw hat on her head, probably to hide the last of the bandages still fixed to her scalp, but none of that mattered to me. The only thing I found myself focused on was the man sitting on the front steps with a can of beer between his legs as he stared at a cell phone screen.

During the ten minutes I sat there watching, I didn't see the couple communicate with each other a single time. No over-the-shoulder comments, no little snide remarks the way people usually do when they're outside in the sun, nothing. Each of them remained within their own world. I anticipated that Laurie's reasoning would be for the sake of safety. Guys like Bailey Saunders had the tendency to explode at the slightest thing, and once they were unleashed, there was no stopping them. Given that Laurie was still healing from a previous attack, I seriously questioned whether she could endure another one.

After I felt confident I knew where to find them if necessary, I restarted my car and vacated the curb. My plan was to drive into a nearby driveway, turn around, and head back the way I came. However, I was caught off guard when Bailey glanced up from his phone, rose from the steps, and walked partway into the yard, his eyes fixed on me.

Something set him off; I just didn't know what. I'm pretty sure he didn't recognize me and certainly not my car, but he still took my approach as some kind of threat. He stood with his hands on his hips, just staring at me while Laurie continued watering her flowers, utterly oblivious to the silent interaction between us.

It must have been panic that made me change my mind about pulling into the driveway.

If Bailey really thought I was somebody, then my turning around might look like someone trying to escape him. Would he jump in his Durango and chase me? Maybe he would take his suspicions out on his girlfriend. I couldn't risk either, so I continued driving, keeping my eyes straight ahead as I drove through the intersection. I kept my eyes on the road for as long as possible before he disappeared from view, but he never moved; his gaze was fixed on my car like a suspicious predator.

Only when I saw the house in my rearview mirror did I breathe again, and thank goodness that man was finally out of sight. In those fleeting seconds, my heart raced, pounding in my chest, and I felt as though my head might burst. I think at that moment, I truly feared for my own life.

I found myself questioning whether this involvement was really worth the trouble. I understood that only time could provide those specifics. Each and every time you get involved with anyone's life, you're never the same person as before.

Chapter 25

I had to confront the stark reality that I would probably never see Laurie Sumner as a patient in the hospital again. And If I did see her there again, it would be as a corpse down in the morgue. Victims like Laurie didn't get second chances with guys like Bailey Saunders in their life. I'd seen too many people hurt, and it consistently ended the same way, injured, beat up, or no longer kicking. Over 25% of deaths occur within the confines of a hospital emergency.

For the next few days, I worked on devising a plan that would avoid my direct involvement with the man, unlike what happened with Douglas Randall. I needed to identify any potential vulnerabilities Saunders might have. Right from the start, there was no way I was going to put on a wig and try to get close to that guy. He might have a spot hidden away in the desert where he discarded various bodies after using them for his own purposes.

I couldn't locate any social media profiles for either Laurie or Bailey. Neither of them had one, which made trying to get information about them so much more complicated. I often wondered how private detectives got any work done back in the days before the internet.

Bailey Saunders wasn't my only problem. I had another issue in my life, and this one was a lot closer to home, or so I thought. It was Donnie. Despite several days passing since our brunch at The Silver Lining, I couldn't shake the uneasy feeling that there was more to him than meets the eye. That off-the-cuff remark he'd made about me being at the establishment on the night Brian Hurst died wasn't one I could dismiss quite so easily. It just didn't make sense.

The more I recalled that evening, the more I was sure that he wasn't there that night, and I would know. I got a pretty decent look at the people in the area, not that there were many to start with. There were two women at the bar, two others in a booth, and Brian Hurst himself. Then there was the bartender, plus me and my friends. Plus, the lonely guy sitting at the outside end of the bar, away from the two women. But he was a lot older than Donnie, and even if he'd worn a disguise, he couldn't shrink his body. That older man would have struggled standing upright in a stiff breeze.

Call it a guilty conscience, if you will, but I decided that I needed to find out one way or another, and the only way I knew how was to try and sneak a look into Donnie's house without his knowledge. We definitely weren't at the key exchange stage of our relationship, and I had two choices. Break in when he wasn't home, or gain entry under false pretenses and see what I could find.

I don't think I could have broken into his house. Even with all of the bad things I'd already done. I wasn't prepared to turn myself into a known criminal and start throwing in a few extra offenses for good measure. That left me with the second option, which meant I needed to search his place while he was home.

To try and make it work, I ended up asking him out on a date to a local restaurant for dinner. Just the two of us, on a Friday night when I'm not at work. He accepted, of course, although he did make a joke about me being the one initiating a dinner date.

"Isn't that something a man is supposed to arrange?"

"Well, how long do you expect a girl to wait?" was how I answered him, and we both laughed it off.

I decided to go a little overboard if you must know. Usually, I would have thrown on some random dress and even gone as far as a bit of makeup. Not that night. That night, I wanted him to ask me to come back to his place, and the only way that would happen was if I hinted upfront that he might actually have a chance to get lucky. We'd had some good eye contact and chemistry for the most part. It's not like I'm a complete prude in the matter, but there hasn't been any abundant activity between us. I know it may not have been right, but I suppose I aimed to turn that scarcity to my benefit.

The meal turned out to be a lot better than I expected. I didn't exactly put a lot of research into the restaurant itself. It was Mackenzie who suggested the place to me when I told her about my plans. She told me that she'd been there twice and, every time, found the steaks to be some of the best. Knowing how much Donnie loved his meat, it seemed like an easy choice for me.

When we got back to his house just after ten that night, we spent an hour or so sitting on his back porch with a couple of beers. It was painful to reflect on the true reason I was there, especially since I was genuinely enjoying myself. I felt a deeper connection with him than I had in ages, and that really mattered to me.

After a wonderful evening, I ended up staying the night. We headed to bed just before midnight, and like a true gentleman, he simply wanted to hold me close. This gesture deepened my feelings for him, and soon, I drifted off to sleep with my head on his chest. Sadness and regret came over me when I first heard his light snores. I nearly violated every dating rule imaginable by my actions. I potentially exploited myself to achieve my goals, manipulated the situation in order to spy, and hated myself even more because my job wasn't done.

I waited patiently for more than an hour before I finally risked moving. He did feel me lift my head and tried to reach out to me. But it was nothing more than a sleepish attempt, and when he missed me, Donnie rolled over and continued snoring. That was just the signal I needed to get started. Moving as slowly as I could, I carefully worked my way out of bed, keeping my torso absolutely still while manipulating my feet onto the floor before finally sliding out.

Once I was up on my feet, I stood my ground for at least another five minutes and listened to those same snores, making sure their repetitiveness didn't conceal someone pretending to be asleep. If he caught me, I knew there would be questions that I'd be unable to answer.

I steadied my breath, instinctively scanning the corners for movement, my heart pounding as I weighed my next move carefully. I stood there and suffered in silence.

Instead of five minutes, I ended up waiting ten, ten long minutes, standing in near-dark conditions, listening to a man snoring his way through deep sleep. Only when I was absolutely sure that he was really asleep did I dare continue with my plan. With my cell phone in hand, I made my way out to the kitchen first, found his wallet, and began to work my way through each compartment.

Using the flashlight on my phone, I studied each card, and nothing appeared out of the ordinary. They all matched the name on his driver's license perfectly; his address was on there too. He even had a couple of Tangem cards for his cold-storage crypto wallets, which he showed me during my first visit to the house.

One of the spare rooms remained completely empty, while the other had a couple of boxes that only held a few books and a couple of model cars. The living room had a few photos of himself with some of his family members, mostly of his father, who passed a couple of years earlier, and his estranged son from a previous marriage. Again, nothing really out of the ordinary.

When I was sure I wouldn't find anything else, I returned to the bedroom and was about to climb into bed. It was then that I noticed the dark shape in the walk-in closet, possibly the prime spot for concealing hidden secrets. I wasn't sure whether to chance taking a look, but that was when my imagination got the best of me, telling me something I already knew. The greatest prizes come from the biggest risks.

I quietly sighed to myself when I knew I wasn't going to let the opportunity pass me by. Donnie continued snoring in that same slow and steady rhythm, and figuring it was now or never, I crept into the middle of that dark shadow before slowly closing the door and turning on my phone's flashlight.

The one thing I noticed almost immediately was the sheer amount of clothes the man had on hangers suspended the entire width of the closet rod. Up on the shelves stood a couple of boxes that I carefully reached for. I took my sweet time as I lowered it to the floor and worked my way through the contents.

An hour was how long it took me to realize that the man had no secrets. And if he did, they weren't located in that house. When I slowly climbed back into the bed beside him, I wasn't quite sure whether I was relieved to find nothing or frustrated at the lack of answers. After all this work, the questions I had all week long were still unanswered.

Chapter 26

When I woke up the following morning to the smell of coffee, I opened my eyes to find Donnie sitting before me with a tray in hand.

He said, "I didn't want to wake you, but I figured you might want some of this," as he lowered the tray to reveal not only a cup of the good stuff but also a plate of French toast!

"You made me breakfast in bed?"

Not only did he surprise me yet again, but the man also had a way of melting my heart every time I felt guilty about doing something to betray his trust. I honestly hated myself for deceiving him like that, and while I admired his hospitality, I thanked him for being so thoughtful.

We didn't spend the day together as I told him that I had arranged a prior engagement with Peg and Mackenzie. Donnie had to take a drive down to Fort Stockton to meet up with an investor interested in some crypto wallets that they were building. I didn't really understand much about it, but we agreed to catch up on the Monday afternoon before my shift started at the hospital. Little did he know I lied.

I felt so bad driving away from his house. But it wasn't like I could come right out and tell him that I would actually be trading my car in for a new one that wouldn't be recognized by a convicted killer, who I was in the process of stalking in the hopes of killing him. Yes, that was my plan for Saturday. I couldn't exactly use the Civic around Saunders, not after the way he reacted the last time he saw me driving past his house, and I figured I was overdue for a new car anyway. The old girl had served me well over the years, but I wanted something new. Perhaps the fact that I drove the car to Lubbock also had a little something to do with me finally wanting to get rid of it.

Feeling a kind of urgency for the car, I ended up buying one from a local dealer who just happened to be somewhat related to me in a roundabout kind of way. His mother was close friends with my grandmother back in the day, and we used to spend time together during occasional visits to each other's homes. Greg gave me a great deal on a 2022 Rav 4 and gave me just over $5000 for the Civic, a price that was nearly spot on what I discovered during my price research.

The changeover took just a few hours, and by three that afternoon, I was the proud owner of a car nobody in the world could positively identify as being mine, least of all Bailey Saunders. Without needing to go back home for anything, I ended up driving straight from the dealership to Laurie Sumner's house, this time taking care to park a little further away.

The Durango was parked in the driveway just like the first time I'd spied on the house, and I figured it was a small win considering the alternative. What I didn't know was how long I would be sitting there waiting for something to happen, especially since I had no clue as to what I was looking for. All I knew was that I felt a sense of guardianship over Laurie. Is that what you call it? A protector but someone who didn't make their presence known, kind of like a guardian angel. What frightened me the most was not being there if things really kicked off and her dying because of my lack of response time.

Two hours was how long it took for Saunders to finally emerge from the house. I'd been lazily scrolling through the internet, wasting time being bored out of my mind, when a distant scream brought my attention back to the moment. I looked up in time to see Saunders slam the door closed behind him before punching it and yelling something else.

"Keep walking, asshole," I whispered to myself as I watched him teetering at the top of the first step. I made up my mind to intervene if he dared go back inside, but thankfully, it didn't come to that. I did make a mental note to look into getting a gun for myself though. I wondered what the hell I would do if I ran into the house after him.

"You wouldn't, idiot," I told myself, and that was when Saunders walked down the steps and jumped in his vehicle.

Dusk was already well underway as I started my engine and waited for him to disappear from view before pulling away from the curb. I reached the intersection, turned left, and saw him turn onto the main road a couple of hundred yards up from me. The feel of the gas pedal responding to me brought a grin to my face. The Rav maintains a lot more power than my little hatchback. It quickly sped up and reached the intersection a few seconds later, and once we were on the main road, I made sure to keep enough distance between us.

Again, I wasn't sure what it was I was hoping to find by following him. This wasn't some overzealous kid with a bad attitude like Douglas Randall or even Kane Nazif. Those two had been nothing more than spoiled teenagers compared to the man I was now tailing, and if he turned on me, I had no doubt that it would be my demise. I was undoubtedly treading on thin ice; a single misstep could lead to deadly consequences. I needed to exercise extreme caution.

His first stop was a random house off 42nd Street in Newell. At first, I thought I had another serial cheater on my hands. But shortly after walking into the home, Saunders emerged behind another guy, and the two of them spent the following hour on the front porch drinking beers. Nothing for me to use.

When he left, we again drove for almost ten minutes before he pulled into a parking lot that accommodated a food truck. A small group of guys sat at two tables, and Saunders joined them as he chowed down on what looked like a hotdog and fries. Again, it turned out to be a complete waste of time in terms of finding something to use against him. Here I was, just sitting back, watching some beefcake shove fries in his face.

An additional hour went by, and as some people vacated, new ones arrived in what seemed to be a continuous cycle of socializing. Saunders stuck around long enough to order a second meal. After he finished, he slapped his hands back and forth on each other, shaking off the salt, then wiped his face and decided to move on once more.

The next stop turned out to be another suburban house; this time, his entire demeanor changed. The aggression all but disappeared when he climbed the steps up to where an elderly couple sat together on a couch. Saunders leaned down and kissed the man on top of the head while the woman got a kiss on the cheek. I didn't need to get close to know that they must have been family to him, perhaps even his parents. I remember seeing their faces in one of the news articles but couldn't be sure they were the same people.

Donnie sent me a message while I was sitting on the side of that road, informing me that he would be spending the night with his friend, who offered him the spare room. Apparently, the pair had spent most of the day working on their little project together and had lost track of time. I texted back, telling him to have a wonderful night, and also thanked him for the previous evening. When he sent back a red love heart, I paused to send a reply.

Love. It wasn't something I had been searching for, and now that it appears to have found me. I wasn't sure whether I was ready for it, especially with these situations I had gotten myself caught up in. Love often complicates situations because it requires open communication and empathy, not to mention trust… If I acknowledged this symbol of love, would I be prone to making the situation worse? It's not like I can break down my problems to someone else.

I ended up not responding at all. His message was a reply to my message, so I figured someone had to have the last word, right?

Why did it have to be me?

Keeping the screen awake, I looked up at the house to make sure I hadn't missed anything. Saunders remained seated on the chair next to his parents and didn't appear to be planning to leave. I took the time to stare at the love heart, an emoji I had seen countless times before but now held some kind of power over me.

Saunders ended up leaving his parent's house around 9:30 that night and I ended up following him all the way back to Laurie's house. With night truly over the city, the house looked to be lit up with almost every light turned on. None of the windows appeared to have their curtains drawn, and I could see straight into each of the rooms, which only served to further exasperate the situation for me. Sitting on the bed in one of the rooms was Laurie, holding a book, and sitting beside her was a small boy aged somewhere around four or five. It appeared that Laurie Sumner wasn't the only one living a nightmare. So was her son.

Chapter 27

For me, seeing that little boy changed everything. Sure, I'd dealt with mothers of small children before, but none of them compared to the volatility of Bailey Saunders. It wasn't adding just another victim into the mix. For me, it took away the most precious commodity of all...time. Now that I was effectively working to save two lives from this monster, the urgency multiplied to an unprecedented level.

Despite knowing about the boy, I still couldn't for the life of me think of a way to end the man, not without placing myself directly in harm's way. There comes a time when you need to grow some balls when playing with fire, but it isn't as simple as that. If I owned a weapon and barged into a situation, shot the perpetrator dead on the spot, and then moved on to someone else. How quickly would my luck run out before the authorities took me into custody to face multiple murder charges?

No, what I needed was a carefully laid-out plan that ensured not only the survival of the victims I fought to protect, but also kept my own longevity intact. That was how I managed to terminate the previous men, or anyone else who crossed my path. I intended to handle these problems one at a time, starting with Bailey Saunders. I had to ensure I stayed under the radar in order to keep assisting those who the system ignored. I'm sure some police are willing, but they needed individuals to confess, write a report, and sign statements. Naturally, not a lot of people come forward when they fear for their lives at home.

I considered spending most of the Sunday again trying to follow Saunders around, but daytime proved another challenge, one that I didn't want to take. Throughout the day, circumstances can shift unexpectedly. When a car follows someone for too long, it could start attracting unwanted attention, making it unmistakably obvious, like a sore thumb. The only thing he might notice at night would be my headlights, unless he couldn't pay attention because his vehicle was filthy, and he couldn't see through the windows. Despite having a new car, I wasn't prepared to reveal to the man what I was driving.

Instead of going out, I ended up staying in for the day, spending the time on the laptop trying to find some other way to get rid of him that didn't involve outright killing. The words and statements I wanted to google would have raised red flags for anybody monitoring search engine traffic, or at least that's what I thought. Instead of asking things like how to kill someone from a distance, I changed the wording to *accidental deaths in the home*, and *unexpected deaths outside the house*. What I found were endless tragedies of people who had met their maker in more ways one can only shake their heads at. I was looking for some inspiration similar to how a thriller author seeks out unexpected twists and turns.

Unfortunately, four hours on my couch with the laptop on my lap didn't help, and I ended up more frustrated than ever before. The only two options I continuously kept thinking about were a possible traffic accident, not something I knew how to set up, or going to the extreme and hiring a hitman. I seriously considered the latter to such an extent that I actually began to search how much one might cost. The amounts I came across were certainly beyond what someone earning a nurse's salary could afford.

When I slammed the laptop shut in frustration at around five, I considered messaging Donnie to see if he was home yet and maybe he'd want to meet up somewhere for a pizza. I figured I'd just go in the kitchen and prepare something. I barely picked up my phone to take it with me when it rang; a little startled by the noise, I answered it like a reflex action.

"Hey, Liz," Peg said from the other end, sounding more than a little flustered. "I'm glad I caught you. Hey, do you want to work tonight? I've had two people call in sick, and another is apparently on leave." She lowered her voice when I didn't answer immediately. "I'm really desperate."

I could have said no, and she wouldn't have been insulted in the least. We both knew she had a job to do. There's a bonus for snagging an extra shift. Cha-ching in my bank, baby! I'd rather make time and a half versus the base rate. Maybe I should have said no, but the truth is, I actually wanted a distraction from the mind-bending possibilities of Bailey Saunders continuously tormenting me.

"Sure," I said. "I'm on my way."

"Thank you. See you soon."

She hung up before I could respond, and I smiled at the thought of her silently cheering as she placed the phone receiver back into the cradle. Texting Donnie ultimately left my mind as I turned my attention to getting ready for work. Aside from a few snacks, I would need coffee...lots and lots of coffee.

Even though I was called late for the night shift, I still managed to arrive at the hospital in time for our usual shift change. Peg was covering for a few people and was working a split shift. I felt sorry for her, and I made a mental note to bring in an extra coffee to help keep her awake.

What I was hoping for when I agreed to the shift was a quiet Sunday night, and for the first half, it was. Half the rooms stood empty, and we'd only received half a dozen patients via ambulance by the time the clocks struck midnight, but that was when everything changed, not just for the ED but also for me personally.

The nurse's station had received a radio report to expect a child in a few minutes. These pre-alerts helped ensure that critical patients received timely care. Half of the staff took off to prepare the operating room from the details and specifics of the relayed message. I kept my eyes on the camera screens, looking back and forth from the patient monitors. Soon enough, the ambulance arrived and began transport into the building.

The moment the paramedics burst through the doors pushing their trolley, the commotion immediately echoed throughout the hallways. When I heard the shouts for assistance, I met the paramedics halfway down the corridor.

My focus was on the lead paramedic calling for people to clear the way so she could direct the trolley through the next swing doors leading into the operating rooms, which was why I didn't see a woman running alongside until she nearly passed me. It was Laurie Sumner, her face ghostly white as she struggled to keep up with the paramedics. On the trolley, her son lay unconscious, the left side of his face sporting the kind of bruise I'd seen too many times before.

When I say that it took every bit of strength for me not to grab her and demand to know where Saunders was, you better believe me. I was so angry that my fingers shook with unbridled rage, the pressure valve inside me ready to explode. With me not assigned to help in surgery and having no other patients at that moment, I took it upon myself to look after the mother, who looked close to passing out. The way she kept calling her son's name just about broke me, as well as the flood of guilt rushing through me for not acting quickly enough.

"Laurie," I said, summoning all the calmness I could as I gently touched her face and directed her attention to me.

"Laurie, listen to me. Aiden is going to be alright. Right now..."

"I SHOULDN'T HAVE LEFT HIM," she cried, her sobs loud enough to echo back to me from the corners of the room.

"Laurie, you have to calm yourself. Laurie, Laurie, look at me," I said, repeating the same words over and over until she finally began to respond. When her sobs began to quieten, I led her to a bank of chairs and sat the both of us down. "Aiden will be fine. He's with the best doctors in the state right now, and they will do everything they can to help your boy."

What I didn't tell Laurie, and what I found out, thanks to one of my colleagues, was that the situation was a lot worse than anticipated. Little Aiden had suffered a burst blood vessel in the brain, the bleed effectively creating pressure that could ultimately kill him. The surgeons working on him raced against the clock to save his little life as they fought to ease the pressure and stop the bleeding.

I waited an hour before I finally gave in to my own pressure, the kind no sane person could control. The anger came and went in waves, but rather than dissipating over time, it only seemed to increase. If I didn't do something to blow off some steam, who knew where my own sanity would end up? Only when Laurie finally stopped crying altogether did I work up the courage to confront her about the problem she'd been living with.

"Laurie, was it Bailey who hit Aiden?"

She didn't answer at first. Actually, I don't think she really heard me, not until I reached for her shoulders and pulled her around to look at me. I said, "Tell me if this was Bailey," needing to grit my teeth to keep myself from shouting. She stared at me, her eyes wide with fear as her lips began to tremble. "Laurie, tell me," I repeated.

"Please, he's crazy. He'll kill me if he knows I talked to you."

"Where is he," I asked, finally feeling my resistance disappear as my true self started to emerge. She didn't answer. "Is he at your house?" She hesitated again, but after a few seconds, she finally nodded. "You stay here and wait for your boy to come out." I leaned closer to her and whispered, "He's going to be just fine."

I got up and walked out of the room before I could change my mind. Instead of heading to the nurse's station to phone the police, I took a left at the junction and went into the medicine room, where we kept all of our necessary drugs. After looking through a couple of cabinets, I found what I was looking for. Playtime was over.

With a bottle of Ketamine anesthetic in one pocket and a 30ml syringe in the other, I grabbed my keys out of my locker and left the hospital for what I expected to be the last time. By this point, my anger had turned to full-on rage, and giving my life to save anybody else who might suffer at the hands of Saunders was something I seriously considered.

No, not considered, but prepared for...

I barely felt one of my nails snap when I missed the door handle of my car, my body running purely on adrenalin by this point. All logic had left me, and I was still thinking that fate would protect me. I jumped in the car, slammed the door shut, and filled the syringe to the very limit. This would be a dose fit for a killer.

Once I started the car, I turned for Laurie's house, ignoring every set of lights I came across. Given the hour of the night, I was lucky enough not to end up smeared across the front of some truck coming the other way. In less than ten minutes, I had gone from sitting next to yet another distraught mother to pulling into the driveway of her home, ready to end that son of a bitch who might have killed her son.

Probably drawn to the front of the house by my headlights, I saw a shadow appear in one of the darkened rooms. Leaving my engine running and the headlights on, they lit up just enough of the house to highlight Saunders when he came out of the front door. Once I pulled the cap off the needle, I jumped out of the car, locked eyes with him, and walked toward the house.

"The bitch from the hospital," I heard him say.

"What's the matter? Did that little punk die?"

He began walking down the steps and probably expected me to slow down or even stop well before reaching me. Maybe that's why his guard was down. I didn't delay. Instead, with just ten feet between us, I broke into a sprint, my scream growing with each step. During those final few feet, I pulled the needle back and watched Saunders flinch in surprise, my sudden rush catching him completely off guard.

"What the -" he cried out when I kicked off the ground at the last second. Continuing to scream, I swung my arm hard, aiming the needle for the center of his neck, and prepared to press the plunger.

In my mind, the needle hit its mark and plunged deep into the soft meatiness, and I pushed all 30ml of the anesthetic into his system. I envisioned him pulling back when he realized what I had done and began staggering around as the overdose went to work.

If only that's how things had played out.

Instead of me swinging my arm around enough to stick the needle into him, Saunders caught me in mid-air almost as quickly as catching a ball. Not only was he fast, but he had the strength of ten men and easily held me up as my short flight came to an end. I continued screaming, desperately thrashing my arms and legs wildly around, hoping to break free. He squeezed my wrist intense enough for the pain to sink in, and just when I was sure my bone was going to snap in half, I let go of the syringe.

"Good choice, bitch," Saunders snarled, kicked my weapon of choice away into the shadows and dropped me to the ground. To add insult to injury, he threw a front kick with his right leg, striking me hard in my chest with his big boot, knocking every last bit of air from my lungs.

I gasped, felt heat rip through my chest, and began coughing through reflex alone. With no air in my lungs to help, I started gasping for what felt like my very life.

"Say goodnight," I heard Saunders say, and when I looked up, I saw him pull a pistol out of his jeans.

Time slowed as I closed my eyes, waiting for the explosion that would bring my sorry tale to an abrupt end. In that instant, I wondered whether the four men would greet me on the other side, all of them ready to claim their revenge on the one who stole their lives from them. It was the ending I had been expecting.

When the gun fired a single round, the thunderclap almost right above my head; I waited for the pain to announce my death. Instead, I heard something dull thump on the ground next to me, and when I opened my eyes, I saw Bailey Saunders lying on the ground beside me. His gaze fixed on mine, his eyes open wide enough for the whites to dominate his stare. Within seconds, the deathly glaze I had seen too many times already began to replace the final remnants of life within them.

Shocked, I spun around only for the world to suddenly crumble around me as I looked up into the face of Donnie Marlow. He still held his gun outstretched, the barrel aimed down at the corpse of the man who almost killed me. Donnie walked up and held his other hand down to me; with a panting breath, I grasped his hand, feeling a rush of hope and judgment as the weight of uncertainty began to set in. A tight feeling gripped my stomach as I confronted the reality that had the potential to alter everything. My relief was intertwined with a profound sense of dread, making me wonder if I was really prepared for what was to come.

Chapter 28

I barely got on my two feet before the first sirens pulled up out the front of the house. Within seconds, more showed up, and before I knew it, a sea of red and blue lights covered the entire intersection. Mixed in with the patrol cars, a couple of ambulances also showed up, and the paramedics were the first to confirm that Bailey Saunders was dead.

For me, the surprises didn't stop coming, especially when I heard one of the officers call out "Ranger Howell," a man who I've always known as Don Marlow. When he finished talking with the cops and explained the situation, he approached me while I was sitting on the front steps, trying to catch my breath. I expected him to apologize to me for lying, maybe to ease into his explanation, but that was wishful thinking on my part.

"We have to talk," was all he said, and after helping me to my feet, he had me turn off and lock up my Rav4, leaving it in the driveway. Donnie led me over to his car, where he held the door open and gently closed it once I was inside.

We drove back to his place in silence, the drive feeling just as strange as the rest of the night. I tried to ask him a question at one point, but he held a finger to his lips and shook his head. Yes, it made me feel like a child, but I didn't dare say so. What frightened me more was not knowing exactly how much Donnie knew about me. As it turned out, he knew a lot more than I expected.

He waited until we were in his living room and didn't begin talking until I was sitting on his couch, ready for whatever interrogation he had planned for me. At first, he just kind of paced back and forth as if searching for the right way to start, but he didn't postpone for long.

"I'm guessing you know that I'm not who you think I am."

"Who are you?"

"Texas Ranger Jim Howell," he said with a matter-of-fact tone.

"And just so you know, I did have feelings for you, Liz. I never expected things to go as far as they did."

"And yet they did," I said, unsure of just how much I needed to defend myself.

"Is it true?"

"Is what true?" I replied.

"You killing these men." He sounded about as confused as I felt, but the question in itself rattled me.

"Donnie...Jim, what are you talking about?"

"Don't lie to me, Liz, for Pete's sake, don't lie to me." His frustration was ready to blow its top.

I actually considered telling him the truth right then and there, but something held me back. Instead, I sat there in silence and let him continue leading me through whatever was going on between us.

"I've seen the footage of you at the bar the night Brian Hurst died. I also saw footage of you at the bar the night Kane Nazif was shot by your friend's new boyfriend. It was actually that killing that caught our attention."

"What do you mean?" I asked. My tone came across as much more dismissive than I intended.

"Damn it, Liz, you *killed* these men. I bet if I look really hard at this kid up in Lubbock, somewhere, I will find evidence of you being there as well." He turned his back to me and paced to the other end of the room before looking back at me. "Please...tell me I'm wrong."

"Donnie, please," I said, embarrassed by my pleading tone, and unable to focus on all these questionable matters at the same time. That was when he pulled something out of his pocket.

I said, "What's that?"

A video, a friend of mine sent me this morning. It's of a car picked up by a security camera at a gas station in Slaton, Texas, on the morning of the young man's death. It's been confirmed as the one driven by a woman who checked into a nearby hotel just a couple of days before. And then a woman left in the late hours, right after a guy took a drink in the bathtub. He shook his head while surveying me, then commented.

"I bet we would all recognize this exact vehicle from the video, wouldn't we?"

At that moment, he determined that my confession wasn't necessary. Instead of pacing, Donnie stopped in front of me and simply stared me down, a look of faint disgust crossing his face.

"Just tell me why."

I said, "If you have to ask me that question, then you don't know a damn thing about who I am, Donnie," my tone lowered to a near whisper. That was the moment I knew the game was up; my role as a guardian angel was coming to an end.

"What does that mean?" Donnie replied.

"Do you have any idea how many victims walk through my doors who never see the inside of a hospital room a second time because their partners end up killing them?" That was when I pushed myself off the couch and confronted him.

"Do you think you are serving the system and delivering justice? Where is everyone when these women get beaten to a pulp in their homes after everyone ignores their cries for help?" I felt my insides ignite as the heat of anger exploded.

"WHERE WERE YOU WHEN THAT PIECE OF SHIT SMASHED LITTLE AIDEN SUMNER HARD ENOUGH TO RUPTURE A BLOOD VESSEL IN HIS BRAIN?"

The tears began to fall, each feeling like a traitorous cancer running out of me. I couldn't stop myself, calling one name after another as I highlighted all the people I had saved. Neena Hurst, her children, Sophia Traiforos, and each succeeding name cried with more magnitude and emotion. Ranger Howell stood before me in silence, his rugged exterior deteriorating the longer I continued until he finally held a hand up to stop me.

"OK, OK, you made your point," he said, his own volume turned down to a minimum as he tried to calm me down.

Feeling more overwhelmed at the fact I had just voluntarily confessed to killing people, I began to feel my world crumble around me. I walked to the window, gazing into the softly lit street outside. Sitting in a prison cell for the rest of my days was what I imagined my future to be, my life of nursing effectively over.

"What are you doing," Donnie asked.

"Waiting for the lights and sirens to appear."

"Why would they?"

I said, "To take me in, of course," and turned back to face him. "Isn't that your duty, Ranger Howell? To take in your suspect after extracting a confession?"

That was when he slowly walked toward me, his eyes continuing to stand guard over whatever emotions he had going on behind them. Poker-faced was what my grandma used to call people like that. There was no pausing at a safe distance from me like I expected him to, nor when he got within arms reach. Donnie didn't stop until he was close enough to sweep me up into his arms. He gently placed his hand behind her head, drawing me in closer until our lips finally met in a soft, lingering kiss.

Yes, I was still confused as all hell, but at least I got to kiss my man for the last time. I expected him to finish kissing me, apologize for what he had to do next, and then call for backup. Imagine my surprise when he did none of those things.

When he eventually pulled his lips off mine, he stared into my eyes and, for the first time that night, began to smile. He said to me, "I knew when I first met you that there was something special about you, Eliza." "I would have never believed that you would turn out to be some sort of avenging angel."

"Is that the official title for a woman who does your job for you, Ranger Howell?"

He grinned again and then broke into laughter. It was the least expected sound I expected to hear, and yet I don't think I had ever heard a sweeter laugh than I did at that moment.

"So, what are you going to do with me now?"

He looked at me for a few seconds as if considering his response, and when he spoke, Donnie again found the words that would surprise the absolute hell out of me.

"I'm going to classify each of the deaths as accidental, of course," he said with that infectious grin of his. "Just like they should have been from the very beginning."

If I can describe to you the feeling of hearing those words, I would say that they freed me. Not in the sense of Donnie letting me go, or the justice system finding me not guilty of crimes I had not yet been tried for, but in a more spiritual way. As I said before, I might not be as spiritual as I need to be, but I believe in God and what He can do for you and through you. But how else can you explain the way I just seemed to be in the right place, at the right time, to take care of the right people? Maybe I had been right all along, and was chosen to fight the battles nobody could. If Fate really is real and I'm right, then I guess my work remains incomplete. So, who's next?